EX RATING

a novel by Natalie Standiford

LB 1837
LITTLE, BROWN AND COMPANY
New York Boston

First Edition: February 2006

Little, Brown and Company

Hachette Book Group USA
1271 Avenue of the Americas, New York, NY 10020
Visit our Web site at www.lb-teens.com

Cover photos from top left,
© Jillian Lochner/Iconica, © Photodisc Red/Getty Images, © Jerome Tisne/Iconica, © PhotoAlto/Getty Images, © Photolibrary.com/Photonica, © Silvia Otte/Photonica, © Jerome Tisne/Iconica, © Henry Hanna/Iconica, © Paul Vozdic/Iconica, © Henry Hanna/Iconica.

Interior created and produced by Parachute Publishing, L.L.C.
156 Fifth Avenue
New York, NY 10010

ISBN: 0-316-15876-3

10 9 8 7 6 5 4 3 2

CWO

Printed in the United States of America

For Julie B. and Beth Z.

1 Radio Stars

To:	mad4u
From:	your daily horoscope

HERE IS TODAY'S HOROSCOPE: VIRGO: The success you deserve finally arrives! Then it spins out of control and crushes you like a tick.

"I'm so nervous," Mads said. "What's that word for when your heart is racing so fast, your breath can't keep up with it and your stomach spazzes out?"

"I don't think there is a word for that," Holly said.

"Spazz-mania?" Lina tried. "Spazzo-nervitis?"

"It feels more like nauseo-spazzmosis," Mads said.

She and Lina and Holly were sitting in a radio studio, about to be interviewed live. They were waiting for Mary

Dando, the host of the show, to give them their cue.

"There's nothing to be nervous about," Mary said. "Just be yourselves. You'll be charming."

"You don't know us very well," Mads said.

Mary had heard about the girls' blog, the Dating Game, from her assistant, whose cousin went to their school. She called the school and set up an interview with the girls, and the next thing they knew, they were in the studio with giant padded headphones on their ears.

"Everybody at school will be listening," Mads said. "There was that notice in the school paper. And our announcement on the blog."

"Everybody in town, too," Holly said. "My mother told all her friends."

"So did mine," Mads said.

"Basically everybody we know will hear this interview," Lina said.

"That was so stupid of us," Mads said. "Why didn't we keep this a secret? I think the nauseo-spazzmosis is infecting my tongue. What if I can't speak?"

"Okay, girls," Mary said. "Ready? You're on in five, four, three . . ."

"Please don't let us sound dopey," Mads prayed.

Mary Dando: We're back with *American Living* on the

National Radio Network. I'm Mary Dando, and today we're talking to the Dating Game Girls. Madison Markowitz, Holly Anderson, and Lina Ozu are tenth graders at the Rosewood School for Alternative Gifted Education in Carlton Bay, California, and they started a fascinating and very popular Web log on their school site called the Dating Game. Hi, girls. Welcome.

Mads, Holly, Lina: Hi, Mary.

Holly: Thank you for having us.

Mary Dando: You started this site as a project for a sex education class, is that right?

Lina: It's actually called "Interpersonal Human Development."

Mads: But that's just a euphemism for sex ed.

Holly: Our school is heavily into educational jargon.

Mads: We wanted to find out who was more sex-crazed, boys or girls. So we put quizzes and questionnaires on the site, but we didn't get enough answers from boys. That's when we decided to lure them with sex.

Lina: In the form of matchmaking.

Mary: So the students fill out a questionnaire about their preferences and you match them with another student for a date?

Holly: Exactly. They can also submit personal ads. But we're really good at making matches.

Mads: Especially Holly.

Mary: And what was your conclusion? Who's more sex-crazed?

Holly: The results were inconclusive.

Mads: But we know the truth. Girls are definitely more sex-crazed.

Mary: Girls? Really?

Mads: Sure. Girls talk about sex all the time. We read about it in magazines. We're always trying to figure out what boys are thinking.

Lina: And gossiping about who did it with who . . .

Mads: . . . and who's still a virgin and who's not, and who's lying about it.

Mary: And you don't think boys are doing the same thing?

Holly: Not as obsessively. They don't think—they just jump in.

Mads: Yeah. Sex isn't on their minds—it's somewhere else on their bodies. [laughter]

Mary: Tell me about the quizzes. What's a typical subject?

Mads: We just posted a new quiz called "What's Your Dating Style?" It helps you figure out if you're more of a hunter or a prey. Some people think they're a hunter, but when you look at their behavior, they're total roadkill.

Holly: And we just started a new feature called "X-Rating."

Mads: Lina came up with the idea when a friend of hers tried to fix her up with one of her exes.

Lina: Only I wasn't interested.

Mary: How does it work?

Holly: It's part of the matchmaking system. Say you're still friends with your ex-boyfriend and you think he'd be great for some girl—

Lina: Just not you—

Mads: For whatever reason, like maybe you're a vegetarian and he's not, but you still think he's a good person, for a carnivore.

Holly: You can write a profile of him, vouching for him, saying what he's like as a boyfriend, what his good points are and what kind of girl you think would be good for him.

Mads: That way, when a new girl goes out with him, it's like he has a seal of approval—from his ex-girlfriend.

Holly: At least you know he's not a complete jerk.

Lina: Unless he is. You can use "X-Rating" to warn people about someone, too.

Mads: But we try to keep it positive, so it won't turn into a venge-fest.

Mary: It sounds like you've learned a lot about teens

and sex from your blog. What's the most shocking thing you've learned?

Lina: Tough one.

Mads: I was shocked at first by how many non-virgins there are in our school. And how young so many kids are the first time they have sex.

Mary: How young are they?

Lina: Some kids said thirteen or fourteen. And they say they did all kinds of wild things.

Holly: But I think a lot of them were exaggerating. Especially the boys.

Mads: Then I got used to the idea, and it stopped shocking me. I'm unshockable now.

Holly: Sure you are, Mads.

Lina: I'm still surprised by how mean some people can be.

Mads: Yeah, like how some boys just want to hook up but they don't really care about you as a person.

Mary: What's the wildest thing you've ever done?

[the girls laugh]

Holly: I don't know if we should say it on the air.

Mads: People think of us as good girls, but if only they knew!

Lina: Mads! Our parents are listening!

Mads: But it's true! Like that time at Sean's party—

Holly: Mads, don't say it! You'll be sorry later.

Mary: Come on, you can tell me.

Holly: Let's just say that that night got out of control.

Mads: And Lina—I mean, she seems so sweet, but she's done some of the craziest stuff—

Lina: Mads, stop it!

Mads: No one will know what I'm talking about. I won't name names, but one time she liked this guy so much, she hid in his bedroom closet [sound muffled because Lina has clapped her hand over Mads' mouth]—

Mary: What about you, Holly?

Mads: She pretends to be sensible, but she's done some wild things—

Holly: Mads, you're the craziest one of us all, so you'd better stop talking or we'll tell all your secrets.

Lina: Your parents will lock you in your room until you're thirty.

Mads: It's true, I like to live on the edge.

Mary: Thank you, girls. This has been fun. We'll have to have you back again to give us more insights into the sex lives of America's teens.

Holly: We'd love to come back anytime.

Mary: This is Mary Dando for American Living. Join us tomorrow when we talk to the author of *Elderlove* about the sex lives of the nation's nursing home residents.

• • •

"Was it bad? Did I say anything embarrassing?" Mads asked. She and Lina and Holly got into Holly's car and drove out of San Francisco. Their town, Carlton Bay, was about an hour north of the city. "I can't remember anything that happened in there. It's all a blur."

"Don't worry," Lina said. "Ramona said she'd tape it. She was hoping to catch us saying something super-dumb on live radio."

"I think she'll be disappointed," Holly said. "I don't think we said anything *super*-dumb."

"No, maybe just normal-dumb," Lina said.

"Normal-dumb," Mads said. "I guess I can live with that."

"You were great today, honey," Mads' father said when she returned home.

Russell Markowitz rubbed his messy Brillo pad of gray hair in a way that told Mads "great" wasn't the whole story. She looked at her mother, M.C., whose smile was wide but tight. M.C., a pet-psychiatrist/playwright, was eccentric and creative and earthy but had the fierce maternal instincts of a she-wolf. Russell, a labor lawyer, was liberal and protective at the same time. It caused some tension in the house. Mads' parents wanted to allow and prohibit everything at once.

"Mmm-hmm," M.C. said. "You all sounded very articulate, and, um, lively—"

"Like you were really having a good time in the studio," Russell said.

"Thanks," Mads said. "It was fun. But I was so nervous."

"You sounded like sluts," Audrey, Mads' eleven-year-old sister, said.

"Audrey!" M.C. scolded.

"That's what you said!" Audrey cried. M.C. turned red.

"I didn't mean it," M.C. said. "It's just—I didn't realize—"

"We're proud of you," Russell said. "We're glad you have an outlet for your feelings. We think you should be free to express yourself any way you like. It's just—"

"If only it weren't so—so—" M.C. fumbled for the right word. "So public."

"She means embarrassing," Audrey said.

Mads couldn't believe this. "Embarrassing! Mom, you're the one who wrote a whole play about how you got ESP! *That* was embarrassing."

"The *Crier* didn't think so," Audrey said. "They said it was 'thought-provoking.' And they loved my acting in it. They said I was—"

"'A twinkling little star in the making,'" Mads finished. She'd heard that quote from the local paper's review of M.C.'s play, *Touched*, about a hundred times too many already. It was taped to Audrey's bedroom door.

"Honey, don't take this the wrong way." M.C. put her arm around Mads. "We're proud of you. We just didn't realize your Web site was so . . . sexy."

"Well, what do you think we learn about in IHD?" Mads said. "Microwave Cookery?"

"Don't worry, honey," Russell said. "We just have to get used to thinking of you as a—"

"A sexual being," M.C. finished.

"Mom! Gross!" Audrey said.

"I was going to say 'growing young lady,'" Russell said. "But your mother is right. No reason to tiptoe around it."

"Maybe we just shouldn't talk about it at all," Mads said. "How does that sound?" She went up to her room.

"We really do think you did a great job, though!" M.C. called up after her.

Mads slammed her bedroom door and flopped onto her bed. Her nauseo-spazzmosis was back with a vengeance.

Stupid parents, she thought. *What do they know?*

I bet everybody at school thought the interview was excellent. Better than excellent. The greatest thing ever! Well, maybe not that great. But good.

Still, her mother's words echoed in her mind. Or rather, Audrey's version of her mother's words: "You sounded like sluts." Did they? Did everybody in town think so, too? Or was her mother being overly sensitive, as usual?

Overly sensitive, Mads decided. It was the obvious choice. The only choice that left her dignity intact.

She logged onto the Dating Game and checked the inbox for new mail. Nothing.

It was too soon, she knew. The interview had only aired that day. But Mads couldn't wait. She was dying to know. What did everybody think?

2 Demon Ex

To:	hollygolitely
From:	your daily horoscope

HERE IS TODAY'S HOROSCOPE: CAPRICORN: To your face, people praise your good work; but behind your back, all they talk about is your visible panty line.

Holly sat in her room with Mads and Lina, staring at her laptop. X-Ratings had poured into the blog since the girls were on the radio, and the girls were busy sorting through them. Because Holly's parents were the coolest about the Dating Game (and everything else), her house was chosen as X-Rating Central. It was Sunday, the day after the radio interview, and judging by the jump in traffic on the blog, a lot of kids had heard it.

"Sylvia completely flipped out," Lina said, referring to her mother. "Completely!"

"I know," Holly said. "She called my mother. She wanted the mothers to band together and do something about us troubled teens. My mother didn't feel like it. Your mom happened to catch her at a bad moment: all out of Nicorette."

Unlike the Ozus and the Markowitzes, Holly's parents had loved the interview. Holly's openness reflected well on their groovy self-images.

"She called my mother, too," Mads said. "Like M.C. wasn't freaking enough already."

"She kept saying, 'I just hope your grandmother doesn't hear about this,'" Lina said. "She still thinks you're a nice girl. You'll feel so guilty if she has a stroke!"

"That's harsh," Mads said.

"Yeah, I can't believe somebody could have a stroke over anything on National Radio Network," Holly said. "It's so mellow." She punched a few keys and pulled up the completed X-Rating forms on her computer screen. "We'd better get started—there are a lot of these."

Your name: *Sage Bernstein*
Your grade: *12th*
Your ex's name: *Holter Knapp*

Your ex's grade: *12th*

How do you know him/her? *school*

How long were you together? *a year*

Who dumped who? *I dumped him.*

Why did you break up? *He loved me too much.*

Are you friends now? *Yes—finally (it took him a long time to get over the breakup).*

What do you think of your ex as a friend? *He's excellent—he's always calling me to see if I need anything or want a ride anywhere, and he brings me little presents like candy or flowers all the time.*

What do you think of your ex as a boyfriend/girlfriend? (What was good and bad about him or her? Vices? Habits? Hang-ups? Family problems?) *He's so thoughtful and sweet, but he can be suffocating. But some girls like that.*

What would a new person have to have (that you didn't have) to make a relationship with your ex work? *She'd have to be really insecure and need constant reassurance that he loves her—because she'll get it whether she wants it or not. Also, I guess she can't be the type who'd get jealous of my friendship with him. Like, if I call him because I need him to do an errand for me, she shouldn't get upset.*

On a scale of 1 to 10, with 10 being the highest, rate your ex: *6*

"Hmmm," Mads said. "Who would be good with a guy like Holter?"

Holly didn't know Holter or Sage well, but she knew who they were. "It sounds to me like Holter still loves Sage and is going along with her 'just friends' thing so he can be around her all the time."

"And she's letting him," Lina said. "Because she can get him to do whatever she wants."

"And torture him," Holly added.

"But why would she want to fix him up with a new girl?" Mads asked.

"Maybe so she can torture Holter *and* his new girlfriend," Lina said.

"Nobody could be that heinous," Mads said.

"Please, Mads," Holly said. "You know better."

"Well, who could we match Holter with, then?" Mads asked.

"Maybe Autumn, if she and Vince ever break up," Lina said. "She and Sage could battle it out for control of Holter."

"Till then, let's put him on hold," Holly said. "Next."

Your name: *Claire Kessler*

Your grade: *10th*

Your ex's name: *Derek Scotto*

Your ex's grade: *10th*

How do you know him/her? *school, plus our parents are friends*

How long were you together? *a year and a half*

Who dumped who? *It was mutual.*

Why did you break up? *We could just tell it wasn't right. We got along really well, but the zing wasn't there. No chemistry. I don't want to get into it too much, but kissing him just didn't feel right.*

Are you friends now? *yes*

What do you think of your ex as a friend? *He's great—almost like a girlfriend. We hang together, go to movies when there's nothing else to do, and I can talk to him about my crushes and stuff. He gives great boy advice.*

What do you think of your ex as a boyfriend/girlfriend? (What was good and bad about him or her? Vices? Habits? Hang-ups? Family problems?) *He's really nice and cute. He's really into music—if you don't like the bands he likes, he plays them over and over until you give up and say you like them. But overall, he's a great guy.*

What would a new person have to have (that you didn't have) to make a relationship with your ex work? *She should love indie rock and hip-hop, and she should be nice and fairly together. Other than that, just chemistry, I guess.*

On a scale of 1 to 10, with 10 being the highest, rate your ex: *10*

"Now that's a good guy," Lina said.

"Wait—I saw a good match for this guy," Holly said.

She pawed through a pile of printouts—matchmaking questionnaires—until she found the one she remembered. "Here—Alison Hicks. She's in ninth grade, she likes music, and she seems sweet."

"It could work," Lina said.

"Let's see if she's interested." Holly forwarded Derek's X-Rating to Alison.

"Look!" Mads said, scanning down to the next form. "Someone X-Rated Sean!" Mads had a giant, long-standing crush on Sean Benedetto, the handsome blond It boy of the senior class. Completely unreciprocated, of course.

Your name: *Ashanti Burke*

Your grade: *11th*

Your ex's name: *Sean Benedetto*

Your ex's grade: *12th*

How do you know him/her? *school*

How long were you together? *two weeks*

Who dumped who? *I guess he dumped me, but he never said anything to me. He just stopped calling, and the next thing I knew he was seeing some blond named Jane.*

Why did you break up? *Guess he lost interest*

Are you friends now? *Kind of. We joke around a lot, and he's nice to me. Once I got over getting dumped, I didn't hate him anymore.*

What do you think of your ex as a friend? *He's okay.*

What do you think of your ex as a boyfriend/girlfriend? (What was good and bad about him or her? Vices? Habits? Hang-ups? Family problems?) *He's so friggin' sexy, it's hard to say no to him. But so many girls like him. His eyes are always straying. He has a huge ego. But on the other hand—so cute!*

What would a new person have to have (that you didn't have) to make a relationship with your ex work? *She'd have to be like a hypnotist who can put him under a spell to control him. Or she'd have to have something no other girl has—what, I don't know. She'd have to be some kind of movie star or something.*

On a scale of 1 to 10, with 10 being the highest, rate your ex: 2 *(I was just writing in to complain about him.)*

"I didn't know Sean went out with Ashanti Burke," Mads said.

"Or Danica Ball, or Shelby Smith, or Ariel Gruber?" Lina said.

Mads scanned through the forms. "Oh my god, there are at least six X-Ratings of Sean here."

"And they're all bad," Holly said. "Listen to this: 'Sean went to the bathroom in the middle of our date and never came back.'"

Lina laughed and read another one out loud. "'Sean asked another girl out in front of me while we were at the Halloween Dance.'"

"Wait—here's a good one," Holly said. "'Sean came to pick me up for a date and hit on my mother!'"

Lina and Holly keeled over laughing. Mads laughed, too, but it hurt a little. She loved Sean's outrageousness. Maybe Holly and Lina thought it was obnoxious, but Mads wouldn't change anything about Sean. Okay, one thing: She'd make him notice her—truly, deeply notice her. If only! Though she'd settle for being superficially noticed, too.

"He's still with Jane," Mads reminded them. Jane Cotham was a tall, beautiful, hip, blond college student who seemed to have Sean in her power. Mads got to know her a little bit that spring when they both acted in a play Mads' mother had written. "He's been with her for a couple of months now. Maybe those other girls just weren't the one. If you know someone's not the one, why keep up the charade?"

"Oh, Mads," Holly said. "He's terrible. He's like the Demon Ex. Leaves a trail of bad feelings wherever he goes."

QUIZ: ARE YOU AN ANGEL EX OR A DEMON EX?

After a breakup, can you stay friends? Or are you a human tsunami, leaving a trail of destruction in your wake? Take this quiz and face the facts about yourself.

1. **After getting dumped, your first move is to:**

   a ▶ cry, then get on with it.

   b ▶ vow revenge.

   c ▶ join a convent (or monastery, as the case may be).

2. **Your ex has a new love. You:**

   a ▶ say, "Good for you."

   b ▶ spread nasty rumors about the new love.

   c ▶ hire a hit man.

3. **You want your ex back. What do you do?**

   a ▶ Beg, plead, and cry

   b ▶ Bribe the new love to transfer to another school (this only works if you're really, REALLY rich)

   c ▶ Kidnap your ex and have him/her brainwashed

4. **Your ex doesn't want you back. You:**

   a ▶ accept it and vow to be his/her best friend.

   b ▶ try, try again.

   c ▶ tell him/her you'll narc about that stash in his/her underwear drawer.

5. **Your ex describes you as:**

   a ▶ a nice person.

   b ▶ a little clingy.

c ▶ a good candidate for shock therapy.

6. You'd never tell your ex's secrets, even after the breakup—except:

a ▶ how his/her mother calls him/her "Pooky."

b ▶ his/her parents' divorce really did a number on him/her.

c ▶ that nose everyone thinks is so cute? Let's just say he/she wasn't born with it.

Scoring:

1. a: 1, b: 3, c: 2

2. a: 1, b: 2, c: 3

3. a: 1, b: 2, c: 3

4. a: 1, b: 2, c: 3

5. a: 1, b: 2, c: 3

6. a: 1, b: 3, c: 3

Add up your total points.

If you scored 6 to 8 points, you're an ANGEL EX, good-natured, no problems. If you could keep a boyfriend, you'd be in great shape.

If you scored 9 to 12 points, you're HUMAN. Breaking up is hard on everyone, and we're not always on our best behavior. It's understandable. But you have the restraint to keep from turning your breakup into World War III.

If you scored 13 to 18 points, you are a DEMON EX. Devil with a capital D. It would almost be worth staying with you just to avoid the mess you make after the breakup, except that the relationship was even worse! Learn to let go.

"All right, maybe Sean *is* a Demon Ex," Mads admitted. "He's not *my* ex, so what do I care?"

"He might be your ex someday," Holly said.

"You can dream," Lina said.

"Anyway, what about the boyfriend you have?" Holly said.

Mads was dating a guy named Stephen Costello. His mother, a sculptor, was exhibiting her work in a big show in Amsterdam and she'd taken him with her. Missing a few weeks of school wasn't a big deal for them. Stephen's family was arty and easygoing that way.

Mads liked Stephen very much, but things were progressing slowly. Maybe a little too slowly. She and Stephen hadn't done that much yet, just made out a little. Anyway, Sean had a way of crowding other boys out of Mads' mind.

"One thing I can say about Stephen: I'll bet he'll be a fantastic ex," Mads said.

A message box popped up on Holly's screen. "Hey, an IM! From Sebastiano."

Lina and Mads leaned in to read the message. Sebastiano Altman-Peck was Holly's nosy locker neighbor in school.

bastiboy: superstar! xlnt interview. rsage now coolest school on planet. my new motto: rsage—live the fantasy.

"Yay," Mads said. "I'm glad somebody liked it."

Holly wrote him back.

hollygolitely: thanx. we weren't too goofy?

bastiboy: no! sexy. school seems sexy now. think i can get thru a whole day w/out my meds tmw, thanx to u.

hollygolitely: glad we could help.

bastiboy: c u at sex academy tmw. u'll be the 3 sex queens of rosewood.

He signed off. "The sex queens of Rosewood," Mads said. "Do you think he's right?"

"I guess we'll find out tomorrow," Holly said.

"You're famous!" Rebecca Hulse squealed.

Holly, Mads, and Lina hadn't made it to the front door of the school when Rebecca Hulse and Autumn Nelson accosted them. Holly stiffened, bracing herself for a veiled insult. Pretty blond Rebecca and bratty brunette Autumn were sort of friendly with Holly, and yet . . . she didn't trust them. Autumn had a self-obsessed blog called Nuclear Autumn, where she ranted and raved about anything that bothered her, and more than once she had publicly blasted Mads, Lina, Holly, and the Dating Game.

"We heard you on the radio," Autumn said. "You were so good. And now we all look like the most sophisticated high school kids in America."

"You think?" Mads said. Holly knew she was nervous. But it looked as if everything was turning out okay.

"Definitely," Rebecca said. "I already got three evites to parties this weekend from guys from other schools. They said to bring lots of those hot Rosewood girls. It won't be a party unless we're all there."

"With me and Rebecca, of course," Autumn added. "I mean, you three by yourselves . . . I don't think you could keep up the illusion of cool. You need backup."

Sebastiano walked in and smiled at the commotion. "I told you," he said.

"Let's go inside," Lina said. "I need to study for a French quiz. . . ."

"You don't need French," Sebastiano said. "You already speak the language of love."

They walked into the red-and-white stucco Spanish-style school building. The halls were just getting crowded. People whispered all around them—Holly couldn't quite catch the words, but the buzz followed them through the hall.

The girls continued toward their lockers. Up ahead, the crowd parted. Holly saw a tall guy with shaggy blond hair and a swimmer's muscled shoulders striding toward them. She glanced at Mads, who immediately lit up. Sean.

"Kid," he said to Mads. He nodded at Holly and Lina. "Friends of Kid. I heard you on the radio. You rocked. I was glad to finally hear somebody tell the truth that everybody knows: Sex totally rules the world. Nice job. All *right*."

Sex definitely seemed to rule *Sean's* world, at least. All he had to do was look at a girl and she was his. Practically.

"Thanks, Sean," Mads said.

"You're welcome," Sean said. "Carry on, little sex chicks. Later."

The intercom speakers crackled to life. The voice of the principal, John Alvarado, broke through the static. Lina called him Rod because he was so stiff, he seemed as if he had a pole up his butt. She'd overheard Dan Shulman, their IHD teacher, call him that, and she passed it on to Holly and Mads. It was spreading fast through the school. A nickname like that couldn't help but stick—especially when it fit the person so well.

"Holly Anderson, Madison Markowitz, and Lina Ozu," Rod said over the intercom. "Please come to my office immediately."

"What could that be about?" Lina asked.

"Maybe he wants to congratulate us on all the good publicity we're bringing to the school," Mads suggested.

"You think so?" Holly said. "That doesn't sound like something Rod would do." In fact, it didn't sound like Rod at all.

"Brace yourselves," Holly said. "I think we're in for some trouble."

3 The Rod Squad

To:	mad4u
From:	your daily horoscope

HERE IS TODAY'S HOROSCOPE: VIRGO: There's only one way to say this: You're in big trouble.

"Girls, I heard you on the radio Saturday," Rod said. "So did everyone else in town, apparently. Which makes sense, since we announced it here at school and in the local papers. Foolishly, it turns out."

Mads, Lina, and Holly were sitting lined up across from his desk. Mads was nervously tearing a Kleenex into tiny scraps. Next to her, Lina's leg jogged up and down, up and down.

"So—you didn't like the interview?" Mads asked.

"Frankly, if I hadn't known the three of you, I would have found it fascinating, if a little scandalous," he said. "And I probably wouldn't have believed half of what you said. But I couldn't listen as a civilian. I had to listen as an educator. And I found it troubling. But what was even more troubling were all the communications from parents I received as soon as I arrived at school this morning."

Mads sank down in her chair. Uh-oh.

"Many parents were very upset to hear what is happening on a school-sponsored Web site. They seem to think we're running some kind of child prostitution ring."

"But you know that's not true," Mads said. "Those parents are overreacting. My parents do it all the time."

"Be that as it may," Rod said. "I don't need the aggravation. Belinda Crocker, the head of the parents' board, insists I take action. So I'm going to ask you girls to remove the Dating Game from the school site."

"What?" Mads cried. "What do you mean?"

"I mean I'm terminating your blog," Rod said. "Your IHD assignment is over. You don't need it anymore. It's time to shut it down."

"No!" Mads cried. "We do need it! It's just getting good!"

"You can't shut us down just like that," Holly said. "Tell us what bothers you, specifically. Maybe we can fix it. There's got to be a way to make everyone happy."

"All right." Rod cleared his throat. "This letter to someone called 'The Love Ninja' drew particular fire."

Rod read from a printout of the blog. "'Dear Love Ninja, I'm dying to have sex with my boyfriend, and he wants to, too. But about once a week my mother asks me if I'm still a virgin. When I say yes, she's happy and leaves me alone for the rest of the week. Here's my problem: If I have sex, obviously I won't be a virgin anymore. What should I say when Mom asks? Should I lie and keep peace in the house? Or should I tell the truth and cause all sorts of unnecessary trouble?—horndog.'"

Rod paused after saying the word "horndog" and looked up at the girls. Mads had to stifle a giggle. It just sounded so funny coming out of his mouth.

"The Love Ninja replies," Rod went on. "'Dear horndog, Whether or not to have sex is your decision, not your mother's. But telling the truth is best. Your mom's got to update her image of you someday. Might as well be now.'"

"What's wrong with that?" Holly, who usually wrote the Love Ninja column, demanded. "We didn't tell her to lie."

"It's the attitude that parents don't like," Rod said. "They feel you're encouraging kids to have sex whether their parents like it or not. They complain that the blog in general encourages sexual activity and could give students ideas they wouldn't have had on their own."

"But that's the whole point," Lina said. "It's give-and-take. Free exchange of ideas. Et cetera."

"These parents need to get a life," Holly said.

"That's not for you to say," Rod said. "You don't know parents like I know parents," Rod said. "It is very hard to make them happy." He lifted a pink message slip to his glasses and read aloud. "'Get that smut off the school site or I'm suing the school, the town, the county, and the state of California! And you personally!' I'd say that reaction was typical."

"Whoever said that is obviously some kind of nut," Mads said.

Rod frowned. Lina kicked Mads.

"It isn't smut, and you know it," Mads said.

"The kids need it. We help their social lives. We help the less fortunate find love. We give them information they need about embarrassing stuff. Like how to deal with zits. And how to keep cool if somebody hurts you. And—"

"And besides that, it's educational," Holly said. "After all, it started as a school project."

"Nevertheless, we can't afford lawsuits," Rod said, "or the bad publicity."

"I thought all publicity was good publicity," Lina said.

"I don't subscribe to that theory," Rod said.

"This isn't fair," Mads said. She had never realized

how much the Dating Game meant to her, but now that it was threatened, she was ready to fight for it. They'd worked so hard on it—and it was a success! It had brought them lots of attention, a national radio interview, new friends, dates, boyfriends . . . and it brought the three of them—Holly, Lina, and Mads—closer than ever.

"You can't just cave in to pressure like this," Mads said. "Give us a chance. If there's something offensive on the blog, we'll take it off. But it serves a real purpose. Don't shut it down!"

Rod sighed. He fiddled with a paper clip on his desk, then he looked at the girls as if trying to read their minds. "All right," he said at last. "I'll give you one more chance. But you'll have to change the content of the blog drastically. Nothing risque. Nothing controversial. Nothing even remotely anti-curricular. Do you promise?"

The girls nodded. "We promise."

"Because if anything provocative winds up on that site . . . if I get one more complaint from an irate parent . . . the Dating Game is history. Do you understand?"

Mads swallowed. How did he define "controversial"? Or "provocative"? Or "anti-curricular"? She was afraid to ask. But she understood the gist. The Dating Game was in big trouble.

4 An Awakening

To:	linaonme
From:	your daily horoscope

HERE IS TODAY'S HOROSCOPE: CANCER: Today you will realize that what you've been looking for was right under your nose all along. Um, duh?

"That so completely and totally bites," Ramona Fernandez said. She and Lina walked down the hall after lunch. "They can't shut you down! What good is a blog if you can't write what you want on it?"

"I know," Lina said. "But what else can we do? At least we can still make matches. And we're flooded with X-Ratings. Seems like everybody wants to unload his or her ex on somebody else."

"I wish I had an ex to rate," Ramona said. "Does Dan count?"

Ramona and Lina had once—not very long ago—been in love with their IHD teacher, Dan Shulman. It was the one thread they had in common—the delicate, tenuous link between them. But, like a spiderweb, it was stronger than it seemed. Ramona bugged Lina at first, and still did sometimes. Ramona was an outsider, a Goth girl who went too far off course, and she tried to tease Lina's outsider self to the surface, which Lina didn't appreciate. But she had to admire Ramona's toughness and honesty.

Ramona had started a cult around Dan. She created an altar to him in her room and wore skinny ties like his over her black clothes every day. Her three friends and fellow Goths, Chandra Bledsoe, Siobhan Gallagher, and Maggie Schwartzman, were so clueless, they were still wearing the ties. But Ramona had stopped, to Lina's relief.

"No, Dan doesn't count," Lina said irritably. "If we start matching students with teachers, the school will *really* go after us."

"I wouldn't rate him that highly, anyway," Ramona said. "Have you seen the way he tags after Camille like a puppy? I've lost all respect for him. He's immature." Their crush on Dan had died the day they realized he was seeing Camille Barker, a French teacher at their school. Dan and Camille didn't bother hiding their relationship, since he was leaving at the end of the year, anyway. Seeing Dan act like a lovesick boy—over someone else—made him less appealing. Lina had always imagined him to be strong and self-contained, different from the boys her age. But now he didn't seem so different after all.

"Immature. Like you're so mature," Lina said. "The girl who worships a guy in clown makeup named Donald Death." Donald Death was the lead singer of Ramona's favorite band, Deathzilla. He had replaced Dan at the shrine.

"Don't dis the Donald," Ramona said. "Anyway, did your parents listen to your big radio debut?"

"Yes. They weren't happy," Lina said. "They think the Dating Game should be shut down. They're afraid I'll be branded as some kind of porn princess when I apply to colleges."

"I'd think being a porn princess would help you get into college," Ramona said. "I mean, it *is* an extracurricular activity. And they say you can make a lot of money at it."

"I don't see you trying it," Lina said.

"So are you going to let Rod kick you around, or are you going to fight?" Ramona asked.

"Fight," Lina said. "Mads is so upset. We all agreed to try to keep the blog the same, as much as we can. We might not post anything too sexy, but *we'll* decide, not Rod."

"I love a good fight," Ramona said. "And I've been looking for a good reason to stick pins in a Rod doll." Ramona was into love potions, spells, and other supernatural stuff that, as far as Lina knew, never worked.

"You need a reason?" Lina said.

They reached the door to the school office, where Ramona sometimes worked during free periods.

"See you later," Lina said.

"If Rod calls in sick with a mysterious ache tomorrow you'll know why," Ramona said.

Lina walked down the hall to the office of *The Seer*, the school newspaper, where she was a sports reporter. She went in and found her friend Walker Moore at a computer terminal, working on a story. She'd been looking for him all day, since the minute she'd left the house. Had he heard her on the radio? What did he think?

Walker looked up from his work, gave her a distracted wave, and went back to typing. He was a lanky junior with pale brown skin and a sweet face. Lina had first met him on a blind date—Holly had matched them on the Dating Game. The date didn't take, but they'd been friends ever since.

Lina sat at the terminal next to him. "Hi," she said.

"'Afternoon, ma'am," he said, still typing.

She sat waiting for a minute, but he didn't acknowledge her any further, so she dove right in. "I need to ask you a favor," she said. "Um, I don't know if you've heard what's going on with the Dating Game—"

He stopped typing. "Heard you guys on the radio," he said. "Pretty funny. You really had that interviewer thinking that you all know what you're talking about."

"What do you mean?" Lina asked.

He batted his eyelashes in imitation of a cartoon girl. "Ooh, we have to beat the boys away with our hockey sticks! We're all having sex in the equipment room at the gym!"

"We never said that." Lina was surprised he'd gotten that impression from the interview. But if he did, it was no wonder her parents were upset.

"I know, I was exaggerating," Walker said. "But you did sound like little junior sex therapists. Rob and I were laughing our heads off." Rob Safran was Holly's boyfriend.

"I'm glad you were entertained," Lina said, but she really didn't mind that they were laughing. After all, she and Holly and Mads had been laughing over it, too. "But the publicity wasn't good for us. Some parents complained, and now Rod says he's going to shut down the blog unless we take off everything that's the least bit controversial."

"But that's all the good stuff," Walker said.

"I know," Lina said. "We're going to fight him. I'm going to write an opinion piece against censorship for the paper. But I can't cover the story as news—I'm obviously biased. Will you talk to Kate about doing a news article?" Kate Bryson was the editor in chief of the paper.

"Sure," Walker said. "But you know, I'm kind of biased, too. I mean, I support you guys."

"Most of the students support us," Lina said. "That's okay. As long as you don't reveal your bias when you write about it."

"No problem. I've been wanting to branch into hard news anyway."

"Sports is heating up, though," Lina said. "Have you seen Sue Bartholomew pitch? We could be looking at the first softball championship in Rosewood's history."

"Nah, they don't have the hitting to back it up," Walker said. "I'll cover the censorship story—that's big. Kate will definitely go for it."

Lina loved talking sports with Walker, as well as newspaper stuff. She felt like a hard-nosed reporter with him. "Thanks, Walker."

"I guess the first thing to do is interview Rod," Walker said, making some notes on a piece of paper. "Then get some reactions from teachers and students, maybe parents . . ."

Lina watched him, the stiff brown spikes of his hair, his long fingers busy with the pen, and a warm feeling washed over her. He was so nice. She asked for a favor, and he got right on it. He stopped writing and looked up, as if aware that she was watching him. He smiled awkwardly. Embarrassed, she smiled back. She tried to look away, but she couldn't. That smile . . . Had he always had such a cute smile? Why hadn't she noticed it before?

"Everything okay?" he asked.

"Sure. Fine." She tore her eyes away from his face and started digging through her bag to make herself look busy. Stupid! Why did she have to let him catch her staring like that?

He went back to work, and she moved to another desk. Her eyes kept drifting toward him. He was typing, *clickety-clickety-click*. So fast! He looked cute when he was concentrating. His forehead crumpled slightly, right between his eyebrows.

Lina stared at the swirling screen saver in front of her, then pressed a key to make it stop. Funny. She felt dizzy all of a sudden. And a little warm. She touched her forehead. Could she be getting sick?

She felt fine, other than this hot, flushed sensation. She placed her hands on the keyboard, ready to type. DATING GAME OPINION PIECE, she wrote, just to get started. She paused. What would be a good title?

Clackety-clackety-clack. She glanced at Walker. *He* wasn't having any trouble concentrating. At the sight of him, her skin flushed again.

You'll be okay, she told herself. *Come on, think!*

She decided to try the stream-of-consciousness method she used sometimes when she felt blocked. If she wrote the first thing that popped into her head, sometimes it loosened her up and ideas came pouring out.

Typing walker crumple forehead clicky clacky cute fingers touch keyboard face honey sweet lips kiss kiss kiss kiss . . .

She stopped. What the hell was she writing? She read it over. *Kiss kiss kiss . . . ?*

Okay, this was weird. Why was she writing about kissing? She was supposed to be expressing her outrage over censorship.

Maybe she really *was* sick. *Focus,* she told herself. *Get a grip.* She started typing again.

A progressive school like RSAGE should set a good example for its students. Suppressing ideas the administration doesn't agree with only makes you want to kiss Walker right now.

She froze. Was she possessed? Why did this keep happening?

Stop being silly, she told her brain. *Concentrate!*

`Mr. Alvarado and the parents' board are making you all melty inside, and if you don't kiss Walker soon, you'll go out of your mind.`

Lina stared at her fingers as if they'd betrayed her. She felt like slapping herself in the face—anything to snap out of this strange trance. But what would Walker think if he saw her slapping herself silly like one of the Three Stooges?

Since when do you care what Walker thinks?

Okay, this was getting out of hand. She pressed her fingertips against her eyes, hoping to cool down. Then she cracked her knuckles. *Back to work. Let's get down to it. Censorship. Serious issues. Start typing. Go.*

`Hey stupid, don't you get it? You like Walker.`

The sentences glared at her. They might as well have been written in red neon. She reread them. *Oh my god,* she thought. *It's true.*

I like Walker.

She let her hands fall, mashing the keyboard.

I like *like Walker.*

"Are you okay?" Walker turned toward her. "You look funny."

Lina touched her cheek. "Me? I'm fine. I thought I was getting sick, but now I realize—" She stopped. *Now I realize I have a huge gi-normous bleeping crush on you!*

Yeah, tell him that, a little voice in her head said, not without sarcasm. *That will really put him at ease.*

"I typed up a few different angles, ways I could approach the censorship story," Walker said. "You want to come take a look?"

"Sure." Her voice trembled. Did he notice? He was actually getting work done. And she was letting her subconscious type out her totally embarrassing lust for him. She deleted what she had written—she hadn't completely lost her mind—and stood slowly. She walked over to him, steadying herself against the various desks and chairs on the way. Then she sank into the seat next to him.

"You sure you're okay?" he asked. "You're all wobbly."

She looked at him. His face was only a foot away from hers. One foot. She could just lean over and kiss him if she wanted to. It would be easy. Just lean over . . .

"Lina?"

"I worked out too hard in gym today, that's all," Lina lied. She didn't even have gym that day. "Muscle spasms."

"Got to watch that," Walker said. "Anyway, I thought I'd go to Rod's office and get his side of the story, maybe call the head of the parents' board and talk to her—"

"And me," Lina blurted out. "You could interview me." It was a chance to be alone with him. She imagined him asking her questions, writing down her brilliant answers, and then falling into her arms. . . .

"Just you? What about Mads and Holly?"

He didn't seem to be thinking along the same lines she was, which irritated her. "I thought it might be easier to talk to us one at a time—"

The bell rang. Lina had to go to her next class. She didn't want to. She wanted to stay there, alone with him in that office, slowly closing up the one-foot distance between their chairs.

But she couldn't. And neither could he. He saved what he'd written and got to his feet.

"Listen," she said. "Why don't we meet at Vineland after school today and talk about it?" Vineland was a popular café in town, a cozy little cottage with a fireplace and a nice view of the valley. A good place to warm things up between her and Walker.

Walker stuffed some books in a backpack and hurried to the door. "I've got chem lab now. We'll talk later."

Lina followed him. "At Vineland?"

He nodded and disappeared into the crowd of students that emptied into the hall. Lina headed for geometry, her pulse fluttering. She felt charged, electric. Walker! She couldn't wait to see him again.

She liked him!

• • •

Lina pulled her cell phone out of her jacket pocket and dialed Holly's number. "Hey, where are you?" Lina asked.

"I'm just pulling into Rob's driveway," Holly said. "Where are you?"

"At Vineland."

"With Mads?"

"No. Alone."

"Alone? What are you doing?"

"Waiting for Walker. I was supposed to meet him here." She paused. "An hour and a half ago."

There was a second of silence on Holly's end of the line. "He didn't show?"

Lina pressed her hand to her eyes. "No. He didn't show."

"Well, so, why don't you leave, then?"

"Holly, you don't understand," Lina said. "This afternoon, I was watching him write and I had a revelation. An awakening."

"What?"

"I like him, Holly. I like Walker."

"Finally! I think he's liked you for a long time."

"Then why didn't he show up when I asked him out for coffee?"

"Boys, Lina. Who knows what's going on in their

dopey little minds? Rob's mother is at the front door, waving to me. I'd better go in now. Call me tonight."

"Okay. Bye." Lina closed her phone and got ready to leave. Walker wasn't coming. Why did he stand her up? Just a day before, she wouldn't have cared, but now . . . Why did things have to be this way? Just once, couldn't she like a boy at the same moment he liked her?

QUIZ: WHAT'S YOUR DATING STYLE?

Are you a Hunter, a Cultivator, a Deer in the Headlights, or Roadkill? Check all statements that sound like you to find out.

❑ **I'm attracted to the cool, quiet type.**
@ ❑ **I believe in love at first sight.**
& ❑ **I wait to get to know someone before I will go out with him.**
% ❑ **I always go after the hottest guy in the room.**
# ❑ **I'm shy and self-conscious.**
% ❑ **I know I'm cute, and I expect the best.**
@ ❑ **I've been in love with the same person for ages.**
% ❑ **I have crushes on lots of people at the same time.**
& ❑ **I believe you should love the one you're with.**
@ ❑ **I believe there's only one true love for each person on earth.**

& ❑ I like people no one else notices.

 # ❑ People don't notice me.

& ❑ My friends tell me I'm nurturing.

@ ❑ I never seem to like the one who likes me.

& ❑ Nobody's perfect, but I'll find a way to make them better.

% ❑ My way or the highway.

 # ❑ I'm flexible—whatever.

@ ❑ If my guy dumps me, I'll do anything to get him back.

 # ❑ My friends say I'm too hesitant.

% ❑ If I get dumped, I just say, "Next!"

Scoring: Count the number of times you selected each symbol. Which one did you pick most? Read that answer section.

Number of %s:

Number of &s:

Number of #s:

Number of @s:

If you chose mostly %s, you're a Hunter. You know what you want and you're not shy about going after it. Just be careful you don't put some people off—not everyone likes your sledge hammer technique.

If you chose mostly &s, you're a Cultivator. You're patient, realistic, and most likely to be happy in love. Just be sure you choose the right person to spend all that nurturing energy on, or you

could find yourself wasting your time with someone not worthy of your goodness.

If you chose mostly #s, you're a Deer in the Headlights. The whole idea of love paralyzes you. Maybe you're not ready yet. Or maybe you're just too insecure. Loosen up and have some fun. If things don't turn out the way you like, it's not the end of the world.

If you chose mostly @s, you're Roadkill. You think you're unlucky in love, but we're not talking about luck here, honey. You choose the worst guys, you approach them in the worst ways, and you leave your heart out in the street for anyone to cover with tire tracks. Make friends with a Hunter and ask her to be your mentor. You need help!

"Help," Lina muttered. "I'm roadkill."

5 Rob's Sister Who's Not Self-Centered at All

To:	hollygolitely
From:	your daily horoscope

HERE IS TODAY'S HOROSCOPE: CAPRICORN: You will make a new friend today, which is good since it's been a while.

"Rob's in the family room," Mrs. Safran said. Holly had only known her a short time but she thought Mrs. Safran looked older suddenly, her cheeks sunken, her skin lined and sallow, the circles under her eyes deeper. "I'm going to lie down for a few minutes."

Mrs. Safran padded down the hall to her bedroom. Holly felt sad watching her. The Safrans had recently divorced, and Rob's father was dating a lot. Mrs. Safran wasn't dating at all. On top of that, Mrs. Safran had spotted Mr. Safran on a date with another woman. Rob didn't like to talk about it, but clearly his mother was taking it hard.

Holly walked through the living room to the sunny family room, which opened onto an outdoor patio. Rob was sitting on the rattan couch with his brother, Gabe, who was living at home and taking classes at Geddison College. Rob was tall and athletic, with thick, unruly brown hair that reminded Holly of teddy bear fur. Gabe looked a lot like him, only smaller, less muscular, with black teddy bear fur. On the floor at Gabe's feet, sleeping and drooling, was the Safrans' big old St. Bernard dog, Murgatroyd. Across the glass coffee table sat a thin girl with straight, lank brown hair—no teddy bear fur here—and plain, geometric features—circles for eyes, a triangle for a nose, which somehow arranged themselves to make a pretty face. She was knitting something out of lime green wool. Holly had never met her before, but she'd seen pictures: Rob's older sister, Julia. She lived in Boston, where she'd gone to college. At least, she did until now.

Rob and Gabe were watching a baseball game on TV. Rob reached for Holly's hand and tugged her down beside him on the couch. "Hey there," he said, giving her a kiss.

"Hey," she said. She waved at Gabe, who was patting a Nerf football. He tossed it to her. She caught it one-handed.

Julia looked up from her knitting. "Hey, Blondie. You must be the girl Rob never shuts up about."

"She's lying," Rob said to Holly. "I never talk about you with my mouth full, or in my sleep. That, I know of. Holly—my sister, Julia Safran."

"Soon to be Julia Safran-McAferin," Julia said. She held out her left hand to flash a big diamond ring Holly's way. "What do you think?"

"She just got engaged," Rob explained. "She moved back to plan the wedding and drive us all insane."

"Congratulations," Holly said.

"What do you think?" Julia pressed.

"It's a little rhymey," Holly said. "Safran-McAferin. Are you sure you want to hyphenate?"

"Not that. The ring."

"Oh." Holly leaned forward to be dazzled by the ring. "It's blindingly beautiful."

"I like this girl," Julia said, dropping her hand. "Rob, she passes."

Holly snuggled against Rob's side. "When's the wedding?"

Julia rolled her eyes. "So soon. Six weeks! Michael—that's my fiancé—wants to take the whole summer for our honeymoon, so we have to get married before Memorial Day."

"That's crazy," Holly said. "You can't plan a wedding in a month and a half."

"I told you," Rob said.

"Luckily she doesn't have a job," Gabe said. "Or she'd be *really* busy."

"Shut up, Gabe," Julia said. "I just graduated from college."

"Almost a year ago," Gabe said.

"There's not much demand for psycho-cosmetologists," Julia said. "It's brutal out there. Wait until you graduate—you'll see."

"I'll have it made," Gabe said. "I'm going to be a cowboy."

"Psycho what?" Holly asked.

"She made it up," Gabe said. "It's not even a real job."

"But it's my dream," Julia said. "I'm going to *make* it a real job."

"She studied psychology," Rob said. "Her thesis was about the psychology of makeup."

"That sounds cool," Holly said. "I bet makeup has a lot of interesting psychological meaning."

"See? She gets it," Julia said. "Anyway, I don't have time for a job now. The wedding is a ton of work. We're having three hundred people."

"Wow," Holly said.

"Michael has a huge family," Julia said. She knitted as she talked.

Holly rubbed Rob's hand. She and Rob had been together for a few months now. They'd fooled around pretty heavily, but hadn't quite gone all the way yet. She'd been hoping for a little time alone with him, but he was glued to the game, and Gabe and Julia didn't seem to be going anywhere. "What are you making?" she asked Julia. She couldn't imagine what would look good in lime green wool.

"A hat for Rob," Julia said. "To spruce him up a little. Don't you think he'll look hot in this color?"

Holly laughed. It would look ridiculous on him. "Better make it big, to cover all his hair."

Julia laughed, too. "Don't worry. I'm making it double the normal size. Like one of those Rasta hats."

From the TV came the sound of a bat cracking. Rob and Gabe leaned forward intently. The ball went foul. Both guys went, "Aw," and fell back into their seats.

"The Giants suck this year," Gabe said.

"So do the A's," Julia said. "So, Blondie, what's your thing?"

"She's a sex goddess," Rob said. "She's involved in a big scandal."

Julia nodded and smiled but didn't stop knitting.

"Impressive. A sex scandal and you're only—what—sixteen? Tell me all about it."

"My friends and I started this blog on the school Web site," Holly began, and ran through the whole story.

"They were interviewed on the radio," Rob said. "And all these tight-assed parents heard it and complained to the principal."

"And now he wants to take us off the school site," Holly said. "We have to remove anything the least bit controversial."

"Which is everything," Rob said.

"Well, not everything," Holly said. "Some of it's pretty tame, actually."

"Does Mom know about this?" Julia asked.

"I didn't tell her," Rob said. "And she's so out of it lately, I figured why upset her."

"You don't think she'd like it?" Holly asked.

"It's hard to tell," Rob said.

"It's true—sometimes Mom's reactions are hard to predict," Julia said. "Like one time in high school I bought a tube top and she wouldn't let me wear it. She actually took it from me and used it to polish the silver. But then a week later she found out my boyfriend and I were, you know, parallel parking, and she was totally cool about it."

"Nobody says 'parallel parking' anymore," Rob said.

"Oh, sorry, I don't know all the high school lingo," Julia said sarcastically. "What do they say now?"

Rob shrugged. "I don't know."

"Your comments are so helpful," Julia said.

"How did she find out?" Holly asked. "Your mother, I mean."

"Read my diary. The bitch," Julia said. "What do your parents think about this big scandal?"

"They're not upset at all," Holly said. "They think it's funny. Curt said, 'That's my girl.'"

"Tell her what Jen said," Rob said.

"Jen said, 'There's nothing like a little raciness to put some zip in your reputation.'" Holly imitated Jen's low, smoky voice.

"She calls her parents Curt and Jen," Rob said. "They're partyers."

"Maybe they should hook up with Dad," Julia said.

The room went silent for a second. Rob had known his dad was dating all along—he'd told Holly about it early on. But Mrs. Safran had just found out, and the wound was still fresh.

"Lighten up," Julia said. "I was just kidding."

"It's true. I think Dad left because Mom's not fun enough," Gabe said.

"Well, who can blame him?" Julia said. "All she does

is get headaches and lie around her bedroom."

"That's just lately," Rob said.

"All I know is, she's no help to me," Julia said. "I thought the wedding would cheer her up, but no, she practically bursts into tears every time I mention it."

"Well, it kind of makes sense, if you think about it for one second," Rob said. "I mean, her marriage just busted up, and you want her to help you plan your wedding?"

"I'm her only daughter!" Julia said. "She should be in heaven."

Rob looked at Holly and shook his head. "My sister. She's not self-centered at all."

"I'm not," Julia insisted. "This wedding will bring much needed sunshine and cheer to our broken home. But I can't do it all by myself. And you two are useless." She dropped her knitting and looked at Holly. "Blondie, you got here just in time. Want to help me pick out a dress?"

Holly straightened up. "Sure." Holly wasn't a fussy fashion girl, but she couldn't pass up a chance to ogle bridal gowns.

Julia stood up and took Holly's hand. "Come to my room. I've got a stack of bridal magazines as tall as Murgatroyd." She stepped over the sleeping dog. Holly moved to follow her, but Rob grabbed her other hand.

"Hey," he complained. "Don't take my girl away.

She was keeping my right side warm."

Julia plucked a crocheted afghan off the back of an easy chair and tossed it at him. "Here's a blanket. Come on, Blondie."

They went to Julia's room on the second floor. Three suitcases lay open with clothes spilling out of them onto the floor. "Sorry about the mess," Julia said. "I just got in from Boston a few days ago. Clear off a place on the bed and sit down."

Holly moved a multicolored tangle of tights and sat on the bed. Julia perched beside her with a *Bride's* magazine covered in yellow Post-its.

"I like the strapless look," Julia said, turning to a marked page and showing Holly a simple white satin gown. "But my arms are like sticks."

"You're lucky," Holly said. "I've got grandma arms."

Julia picked up one of Holly's arms and stared at it. "You do not. You're crazy. Look at this." She rolled up her sleeve and showed Holly her bony arm. "See how the skin hangs loose here? It flaps around like a chicken wing."

Holly laughed. "Now *you're* crazy. But don't get strapless if you're not going to be comfortable in it. Let's see some of the other dresses."

They looked through dozens of magazines, but Julia just couldn't settle on a dress. Every one of them had something wrong with it, however tiny.

"I love that," she said, pointing to a lace slip dress with a blue satin sash. "If only the lace pattern wasn't so flowery."

Holly turned the page. "What about this? It's just satin, no lace."

"Yeah, but I want *some* lace," Julia said. "Just not that kind of lace."

When Rob knocked on the door a few hours later to announce that the Giants had lost, he found his girlfriend and his sister collapsed on the floor, giggling like morons, and the walls of the room plastered with pictures of dresses. Holly had helped Julia narrow it down from thirty possibilities to eight, which was a major accomplishment.

"Great," Rob said. "My sister is spreading her insanity virus to my girlfriend. I'm so glad."

"Holly, if you need advice on bossing him around, come to me," Julia said. "I'm the expert. And I've got a lot of dirt on him, for all your blackmailing needs."

"Blackmail's a little harsh," Holly said. "But I'll take the bossing tips. My older sister was a master, but I made it too easy for her." Julia's sharpness reminded Holly of her older sister, Piper. But Piper had a stronger sense of style, and carried herself with more confidence than Julia, even though Piper was only eighteen.

"Sure you did." Rob reached for her hand and helped her off the floor. "Come on, *Blondie*, I need a little more face time before you have to go home. Can I have my girlfriend back now, Julia?"

"But we haven't found my dream dress yet," Julia said.

"Don't worry, I'll be back," Holly said. In fact, she could hardly wait.

6 Is He Blowing You Off?

To:	linaonme
From:	your daily horoscope

HERE IS TODAY'S HOROSCOPE: CANCER: Are you in pain? Oh, I'm so sorry. But guess what? You deserve it!

"Walker, why didn't you show up at Vineland yesterday?"

Lina found Walker covering a swim meet after school. She was nervous about seeing him. She used to talk to him so easily, but now, suddenly, she felt clammy and tongue-tied around him. She couldn't stop thinking about him and wondering why he'd blown her off. Ramona recommended coming straight out and asking him. It wasn't subtle—and Ramona was no love expert. But it was the quickest way to find out.

Walker glanced up at her and opened his mouth to speak. But then the whistle blew and the 100-meter freestyle started. "Can't talk now," Walker said. "Got to watch the race."

Lina sighed and sat down beside him on the bleacher. The sprint ended about a minute later. Walker jotted some notes on his pad and said, "Sorry—did you just ask me something?"

Lina frowned at the side of his face. Was he really going to make her ask again? She'd be mad at him if he hadn't had such a sweet profile. "Vineland? I waited for you for two hours."

"Really?" He didn't stop writing. "Sorry, I didn't know. I figured you were going to be with a bunch of friends. I didn't think you'd miss me."

"There was no bunch of friends," Lina told him. "I'd planned to talk to you alone. About the Dating Game controversy."

"Oh, right. I'm sorry, Lina."

"I guess it was just a misunderstanding."

"Exactly," Walker said. "It was a misunderstanding."

His words had an eerily familiar ring. In fact, she had said something very similar to him not long ago. He'd asked her to a movie, and she'd assumed it was just a group hang, not a date. But apparently she'd misunderstood him, just as he'd misunderstood her yesterday. Coincidence? Lina didn't think so. She studied him, trying to figure out if he was really saying what he meant. But another race had started, and his attention was on the pool.

"Well, let me know when you want to get together . . . and talk about the Dating Game article," she said, getting to her feet.

Walker ignored her, concentrating on the race. Or pretending to, anyway. Lina returned to Holly and Mads, who were sitting a few bleachers up in the stands. Ramona had tagged along, too, because she had nothing better to do.

"What did he say?" Holly asked.

"He said it was a misunderstanding," Lina said. "He thought it was supposed to be a group hang."

"Weird," Mads said. "That's exactly what you said when—"

"I know," Lina said. "The question is, was it an honest mistake? Or is he punishing me for standing him up before? Which I didn't mean to do, by the way."

"He's punishing you," Ramona said. "The old 'taste of your own medicine' deal."

"Mads?" Lina asked.

"He seems too nice to be that mean on purpose," Mads said. "But it sure feels like déjà vu. I vote punishing."

"Holly?"

"Punishing. But none of us really knows for sure. There's one way to find out, though."

"What?"

"You could ask him whether he really meant to stand you up," Mads said.

"That's too direct," Holly said. "And, anyway, he might lie. You've got to do something that doesn't leave room for misunderstandings and misinterpretations. Ask him out on a date. Make it crystal clear that that's what it is—a date. See what he says."

"He's got to say yes," Mads said, bouncing in her seat. "I know he will! I think he's liked you for a long time. He's probably been waiting for you to ask him out."

"Maybe that's why he stood me up in the first place," Lina said. "To force me to ask him on a real date." Her mood brightened. There was hope. He was just playing hard to get!

"That's giving him too much credit," Holly said. "Remember, he's a guy. They're not usually that clever when it comes to dating strategy."

"You're right," Ramona said.

Lina's mood deflated again. "I hope he says yes. What will I do if he says no?"

"At least you'll know where you stand," Holly said.

"We'll help you forget about him," Mads said. "We're matchmakers, remember?"

"What if he says yes and then stands you up again?" Ramona said.

"He couldn't be that mean," Lina said. "Could he?"

"If he is, he's toast," Ramona said. "I'll make it my business to see that he feels major pain."

"Ramona!" Lina said.

"Stop being so dramatic, Ramona," Holly said. She was impatient with Ramona and her affectations. She didn't understand why Lina let her hang around.

"I don't want anyone feeling pain, no matter what," Lina said.

"You will if he hurts you again," Ramona said. "It's human nature."

"The worst part is not knowing what he's thinking," Lina said. "The uncertainty. Was standing me up an honest mistake? Or is he blowing me off?"

"If you ask him out, you'll have your answer," Holly said. "Probably."

QUIZ: IS HE BLOWING YOU OFF?

He says he's busy—but with what? Is it that he can't see you, or he doesn't want to see you? Sometimes the guy of your dreams really has a legit excuse—and sometimes he's avoiding you. How can you

tell the difference? It's all in the way he handles it. Take this quiz and learn.

1. **You ask him to the movies. He says:**
   a ▶ he'd love to another time.
   b ▶ he's got to take care of his sick mother that night.
   c ▶ movies are against his religion.

2. **He says he'll see you at a party, then doesn't show. When you ask him where he was, he says:**
   a ▶ his car wouldn't start.
   b ▶ he just didn't feel like going.
   c ▶ he was there—where were you?

3. **The big dance is coming. You let him know you don't have a date yet. He says:**
   a ▶ he wishes he could take you, but another girl asked him first.
   b ▶ too bad for you—only losers go to dances alone.
   c ▶ he'd ask you but he's allergic to whatever detergent it is you wash your clothes with.

4. **A friend fixes you up with a cute guy. At the end of the date, he says:**
   a ▶ We should do that again soon.

b ▶ I had more fun than I would have if I'd just sat home alone.

c ▶ I'd love to get together again, but I'm moving to Iceland in the morning.

5. You ask how you can reach him. He:

a ▶ says his cell phone service was cut off, but he'll give you the number when it's working again.

b ▶ says he doesn't believe in technology—but you can mail him a letter if you want.

c ▶ gives you a phone number with a Mongolian area code.

6. You run into him on the street and ask if he wants to go get some ice cream. He says he'd like to, but:

a ▶ he has to get home to baby-sit his sister.

b ▶ he has to get home in time to watch Championship Bowling.

c ▶ he left his anti-cootie spray at home.

Scoring:

Mostly a's: His excuses sound pretty plausible, for the most part. He's probably telling the truth, unless he's a really good liar (sorry, but you can never really know).

Mostly b's: Keep an eye on him. His excuses lean to the lame side, and he might be dodging you.

Mostly c's: Sorry, but he just doesn't like you. Forget about him. He's certainly forgotten about you.

The next day, at the end of the day, Lina spotted Walker again. Standing in front of the school building, talking to some guy. Getting ready to go home.

The night before she'd rehearsed in her mind what she was going to say. She'd even dreamed about it. All day she was jumpy, thinking he'd be lurking around the next corner and then she'd have to muster up her courage and do it. Get it over with.

But he'll say yes, she thought. Why wouldn't he? He'd wanted to go out with her before, when they first met. She'd said no, too preoccupied with Dan to give any real attention to a boy her own age. But that was all over now. She'd changed. Had he?

The guy he was talking to went back inside the school. Walker started down the front path toward the street. She took a deep breath. *Here goes.*

"Walker! Wait!" she called, running after him. "I want to ask you something."

He stopped and turned around to see her. "Hey Lina, what's up? Is this about that interview? Because I don't have time to do it right now—maybe later this week?"

"Um—sure," Lina said.

"Well, see you." He started to walk away.

"Wait—that's not what I wanted to ask you about," Lina said.

He stopped again and waited.

"Um, Walker, I was wondering if you'd like to go out with me this Saturday night," Lina said. She paused to steady her nerves. She had never asked a boy out before. It was scary. Really scary. How would he react?

He looked surprised. Pleasantly surprised. That was good. She pressed on. It had to be crystal clear.

"Not a group hang, just you and me," she added. He blinked. The pleasant surprise on his face was souring now.

"On a date," she said. "To see a movie. Or whatever you want to do."

Her heart was pounding so hard, she could barely breathe. *Please say yes, please say yes,* she prayed. What was taking him so long?

"Thanks for asking, Lina," he said at last. "But I can't."

"You can't?" Now her heartbeat was lighter but quicker, a mouse running a hamster wheel in her chest. "You mean, you're busy?"

"Not really," he said.

The mouse in her chest was slowing down, losing spirit. If Walker didn't clear this up soon, and in a good way, she thought, her heart would stop altogether.

"You can't—or you won't?"

"I—I can't," he said. He looked uncomfortable now,

as if something had come up that he really didn't want to talk about. But what could it be? "It's really nice of you, but I can't go out with you. I'm sorry."

He hurried away, down the path, onto the sidewalk, and down the street. Lina stood staring after him in shock. The mouse in her chest was gone, replaced by the heavy pounding again.

He'd said no. Definitely, unequivocably no. But why? *He just couldn't?* What was that supposed to mean?

Ramona was right, Lina thought. *This really does hurt.*

7 Rod Goes Godzilla

To:	mad4u
From:	your daily horoscope

HERE IS TODAY'S HOROSCOPE: VIRGO: They say what doesn't kill you makes you stronger. But what do "they" know? Who are "they," anyway?

"You guys are the best!" Alison Hicks whispered. Mads, Holly, and Lina were clustered around a table in the library, pretending to be studying history but really reading magazines. Alison sat down with them. They'd set her up with Derek Scotto, based on his X-Rating by Claire Kessler.

"I really like Derek," Alison said. "We're going out this weekend. Claire called me to give me all the inside dope on him. She said I should brush up on obscure rock bands or I won't know what he's talking about. But otherwise he seems cool."

"Let us know how the date goes," Holly said.

Alison got up from the table. "I will. See you."

"She's our third happy customer this week," Mads said. "X-Rating is our greatest invention yet! If only Rod could see how much happiness it brings, he'd never want to censor us or shut us down."

"He'd make us an official school site," Lina said. "Required reading."

"Yeah," Mads said. "He'd keep the site going even after we graduate. He'd get some new IHD students to take over. The Dating Game would be a Rosewood institution. If only he were cool."

"I don't think he cares about *our* happiness," Holly said. "His deal is the parents board's happiness."

"It's the classic struggle of the underclass against the ruling class," Mads said.

Holly and Lina stared at her, then burst out laughing.

"What?" Mads said. "We're the underclass—literally, since we're sophomores—and the administration—"

"We get it, Mads," Holly said.

"We've got tons more X-Ratings to sift through," Lina said. "Want to do it at my house later?"

"I can't," Holly said. "I'm supposed to go check out caterers with Julia."

"She's really got you working for her," Mads said.

"Yeah," Holly said. "It's fun, though. Pretty fun. Most of the time. It's usually fun."

"I'll come over," Mads said.

"Good," Lina said. "That way I won't be tempted to waste the whole evening write sad love poems."

Mads felt bad for Lina. She couldn't believe Walker had refused to go out with her—and wouldn't even give a reason. Not even a face-saving white lie.

The intercom crackled to life. "Will Holly Anderson, Madison Markowitz, and Lina Ozu please report to Mr. Alvarado's office immediately," Rod's secretary's voice said.

Mads looked at Holly and Lina. "Uh-oh. What now?"

"I can't think of anything we've done wrong," Lina said. "We didn't publish any of the dirty X-Ratings."

Like the one by the girl who said her ex-boyfriend liked to do it in the car, Mads thought, her heart sinking. *And only in the car, even though his parents were never home.* She knew enough not to put that on the blog. But could something have slipped through the cracks?

"Hello, girls," Rod said as they sat down in his office. "I've been seeing a lot of you these days."

"If you're sick of us, we can leave," Mads said.

Rod cracked a tense smile. "I wish it were that simple. Do you recall the warning I gave you the last time we met?"

The girls nodded. Nothing controversial on the Dating Game or he'd shut it down.

"Good," Rod said. "Did you understand it? Was it somehow not clear?"

"We understood," Mads said. "Though we might have a different definition of 'controversial' from yours."

"I'm sure you must," Rod said. "Otherwise, I assume an item like this would not have appeared on your blog." He picked up a printout. "I believe this is what you call an X-Rating," he said. "A young man named Dashiell Piasecki wrote it about his former girlfriend, Arabella Caslow. I happen to know Dashiell; he's a behavior challenge. And a frequent visitor to this office."

Mads tried to remember what Dash had written about Arabella. He was an obnoxious jerk, and Arabella had said so in *her* X-Rating of *him*. But his of her hadn't seemed so bad; in fact, Mads had the impression he still liked her.

"I'll skip the preliminaries and go straight to the highlights," Rod said. He read from the printout. "'Arabella is a bangin' chick. And that booty! I like girls with a little meat on their bones.'"

Mads looked at Holly and Lina, shrugging. What was the big deal?

"Mr. Alvarado, all he's saying is that Arabella is attractive," Holly explained. "It's a good thing."

"That's not the point," Rod said. "Her parents happened to see this—I should warn you that since you've received so much publicity recently, many parents have been reading our school site quite carefully. The Caslows were offended by the word 'bangin and 'meat' in reference to their daughter."

"'Bangin' just means she's good-looking," Mads said.

"But in a sexy way, correct?" Rod said.

"I guess," Mads conceded.

"But when he says he likes meat on her bones," Rod said. "Isn't that like calling her a piece of meat?"

"My grandmother says that," Mads said. "'You could use a little meat on your bones,' she says. And the witch in Hansel and Gretel uses that expression. It doesn't mean he's calling her a piece of meat."

"But the witch is fattening up Hansel to eat him," Rod reminded her.

"Was Arabella upset?" Lina asked.

"I don't know," Rod said. "But her parents certainly were. They don't like having their daughter's attributes discussed online this way, and I don't blame them. It's crude."

"But Dash was just trying to say she'd make a good girlfriend," Mads said. "Sure, he's crude, but that's the way he is. It's not our fault."

"Some parents don't want their children to see crudeness at school," Rod said. "I believe that parents have a right to control what their children are exposed to.'"

"But we're only exposing ourselves to ourselves," Mads said. "What's wrong with that?"

"Listen, girls," Rod said. "I refuse to get into an argument with you over this. You were warned, fair and square. Since then, the complaints from parents have only become louder. I have no choice. I'm removing the Dating Game from the school site. I'm sorry."

"But, Mr. Alvarado, that's not fair!" Mads' blood was boiling. He was dumping their blog completely! For nothing! "What good is the site if we can't express ourselves naturally and say what we really think, in the words we normally use? It's—"

Rod cut her off. "Enough. I said I won't argue about it. This is the way it is, period. Please leave my office now." He started shuffling papers around on his desk as if he were busy. Mads felt like spitting at him. She got up and left the office, followed by Holly and Lina.

"I can't believe it!" Mads cried once they were out in the hall. "What are we going to do now?"

"We could move the Dating Game to a site of our own," Lina suggested.

"Or one of those blog sites like Autumn uses," Holly said.

Mads stamped her foot. "No. It's not right. It's the principle of the thing. The Dating Game is a special RSAGE feature. It's only open to us and is protected from infiltration by anyone outside the school. It's part of the community. It brings us all together, gives us a common place to say what's on our mind. That's what's cool about it. And, anyway, this is totally unfair. We can't let Rod and those control-freak parents do this to us!"

Holly and Lina stared at her in surprise. "Wow, Mads, you're really fired up. I've never seen you like this," Lina said.

"We may be kids, but we have rights! They can't tell us what we can and can't write!" Mads said. "There are things we can do. We're not beaten yet."

8 As Usual, Eavesdropping Proves Useful

To:	linaonme
From:	your daily horoscope

HERE IS TODAY'S HOROSCOPE: CANCER: You will solve a mystery using dubious methods. If you don't like what you find out, that's your problem.

"That blows!" Ramona said. "Rod is a total fascist."

Lina and Ramona were walking to the lunchroom, and Lina had just told her how Rod had shut down the Dating Game. She and Ramona didn't agree on everything, but she knew Ramona would be sympathetic to any resistance to authority.

"I know," Lina said. "It's so unfair."

"You're not going to let him get away with it, are you?" Ramona said. "Typical, you three are such goody-goodies. Always doing as you're told—"

"Stop it, Ramona," Lina said. "You're so wrong. We're definitely going to do something. We just don't know what yet. We're meeting tonight to come up with ideas."

"Good luck with that," Ramona said. "Let's sit over there." She pointed to a table in the center of the lunch-room.

"Why this one?" Lina asked as they sat down.

"Because it's prime eavesdropping real estate," Ramona whispered. "Duh. The only thing that makes lunch bearable."

Lina wasn't used to eating lunch alone with Ramona—she ate with Holly and Mads when she could, and Ramona was usually surrounded by her Goth goons. But this after-noon the goons—Chandra, Maggie, and Siobhan—and Holly and Mads all had a history test next period and were huddled in the library cramming. Lina and Ramona were in the same history section, and they had taken their test third period. So Lina was left to eavesdrop with Ramona.

"It's not very polite," Lina said.

"Who cares?" Ramona said. "Neither is gossiping, which is what I believe is going on behind me, if I'm not wrong. Let's zoom in on it with our bionic ears and see."

She cupped her hand to her ear as if it could send out sonar signals.

"We should at least try to not *look* as if we're eavesdropping," Lina said.

"Shh. Tell me who's sitting back there so I don't have to turn around and make it completely obvious that I'm listening."

Lina looked at the group of girls sitting behind Ramona. They were a glossy trio of juniors, all blond or at least blondish: Bridget Aiken, Flynn Hawley, and Rachel Stromm. Flynn was the blondish one, more of a light brown with blond streaks.

"I'm spending the summer in Canada," Flynn was saying. "Aunt Lacey hired me as an intern on her next movie. They're shooting in Vancouver."

"Wait—don't tell me," Ramona whispered to Lina. "Flynn Hawley. She's always bragging about her aunt Lacey. And she goes nowhere without Bridget and Rachel. Right?"

"Right," Lina said. Flynn's aunt Lacey was the famous film director Lacey Kittredge. And Flynn *was* always bragging about her. Lina didn't know her well, but she was no fan of braggarts. Flynn rubbed her the wrong way.

"You're so lucky," Bridget said. "I've got to give tennis lessons at the club again this summer. Yawn."

Lina unwrapped her cheese sandwich. She really

didn't care how Bridget and Flynn were spending their summer. She tried to ignore them, but it was hard because Ramona was busy listening and shushed Lina whenever she tried to talk.

"I was really excited about working on the movie before," Flynn said. "But now, I don't know if I want to be gone all summer. What about Walker?"

Lina's ears perked up. Walker? Yes, what about Walker? Ramona caught her eye. Lina's body tensed as she waited to hear more.

"Maybe he can come visit you," Rachel said. "Vancouver's just a short flight away."

"It will be hard for him," Flynn said. "He has to get a job here, although he doesn't know what yet. . . . Things are just getting good with him, you know? I really like him."

Lina stifled a gasp. Ramona's eyebrows nearly shot to the ceiling. Things were just getting good? Lina knew Ramona could read the question in her eyes: Were Walker and Flynn a couple?

"And we're in the beginning stages," Flynn went on. "I don't quite have him nailed down yet—know what I mean? If we're not more settled by June, I'll be afraid he might meet someone else over the summer."

"But he really likes you," Bridget said. "That's obvious."

"He'd wait for you, Flynn," Rachel added.

Lina pinched Ramona's arm. "Walker and Flynn?" she whispered.

"It can't be," Ramona said. "But Flynn sure seems to think so."

"I already told Aunt Lacey I'd do it," Flynn said. "I can't let her down. I wonder if she'd give Walker a job, too?"

"Are you guys finished eating yet?" Bridget asked. "I've got to get out of here. This place smells like ammonia."

"Yeah, let's go," Rachel said. The three girls got up, bused their trays, and left.

Now Lina and Ramona could talk freely. "How could Walker like her?" Lina asked. "She's so superficial!"

"I thought he was cooler than that," Ramona agreed.

"Maybe it's only in her imagination," Lina said. She knew she was clinging to a thread of hope, but it was all she had left. "Maybe she just *wishes* she was seeing Walker. How can we find out for sure if it's true?"

"Just look out there." Ramona nodded toward the windows, which opened onto the courtyard. Flynn, Bridget, and Rachel bumped into Walker, who smiled and took Flynn's hand. Lina felt like screaming. *He was holding Flynn's hand!*

There was absolutely no question about it: Walker actually liked Flynn.

"Ugh! I can't look!" Lina dropped her head on the table. So that was why Walker couldn't go out with her—and why he was so vague about the reason. He liked Flynn.

"It *is* a horrible sight," Ramona said. "Totally gross."

Lina felt like crying. "You know what kills me? I could have had him. I mean, I think I could have. If only I hadn't wasted so much time mooning over Dan. If only I had realized what a great guy Walker is the first night I met him . . . we could be together now!"

"Well, nobody can blame you for being obsessed with Dan," Ramona said. "You're only human."

"It was so stupid," Lina said. "And now . . . I really like Walker. And I'm afraid I missed my chance."

"Timing," Ramona said. "It's the key to love. I'm beginning to see that now."

"It's everything," Lina said.

"Like, if I'd only been born about seven years earlier, I'd be the right age for Dan," Ramona said. "But on the other hand, I wouldn't be in high school, so I might never have met him. I just can't get the timing right."

"Remember Romeo and Juliet?" Lina said. "They had the worst timing ever."

"Yeah, bad timing can actually kill you," Ramona said. "It's spooky. And now you and Walker—another casualty of fate. Another chance for happiness, missed. Two lives ruined because you couldn't get yourself together—"

"He's got a new girlfriend," Lina wailed. "I'm too late!"

"Probably," Ramona said. "But not necessarily. People break up, you know."

"But what if they don't? Or what if they do but it's not for years and years, when I'm an old lady?"

"Then you and Walker will be old geezers together," Ramona said. "Better late than never."

Lina didn't find this funny. "Ramona, what am I going to do?"

"Don't give up so easily," Ramona said. "You heard Flynn: Things are in the early stages. She's not too sure of him yet. She's afraid to leave him alone this summer. So you've still got a chance to lure him."

"But how?"

"I'll start on some love potions right away," Ramona said. "The hard part is slipping them into his food without him knowing—that's always tricky. But I can manage it. And we'll take it from there."

Love potions. Was she reduced to that? Lina's heart sank. She didn't put much faith in Ramona's abilities as a shaman. She hadn't seen one of her spells work yet.

"This is all my fault," Lina said. "He liked me when we first met, and I pushed him away. And pushed and pushed.

Of course he gave up and went for another girl."

"You can get him back," Ramona said. "If he liked you once, he can like you again."

"I don't know," Lina said. "I really like him as a friend, too. Is it going to be weird between us now that I know he has a girlfriend? What if I just swallow my feelings and pretend nothing's wrong? Do you think we can be friends the way we used to be while he's going out with Flynn?"

"You guys will never be friends the way you used to be," Ramona said. "You never *were* friends the way you think you were. He had a crush on you. You were clueless. End of story. I'm beginning to think guys and girls can't be friends, anyway."

"Yes, they can," Lina said. "I can do it. I'll just put my feelings aside. Be professional. He'll see that I'm cool with whatever is happening, and that nothing he does can hurt me."

"That is a total lie."

"I know that. But he doesn't have to. I've already humiliated myself enough. If I can't have Walker, at least I can have my dignity."

"Dignity? Please. Love and dignity have nothing to do with each other."

"I will rise above," Lina said. "You'll see. Tomorrow is Spring Sports Saturday. That will be the ultimate test."

Spring Sports Saturday was like homecoming except it happened in spring instead of fall. Most of the sports teams had major contests, and Lina and Walker would be working together all day, covering the games for *The Seer*. If things were awkward between them, it would be a long, long day.

"I'll show him that I'm above jealousy. Sure, I asked him out and he said no. He has a new girlfriend. That won't bother me. I'm a journalist. I'll do my job no matter what. And nothing he does can bother me. Because I'm already over him."

Ramona snorted. "He won't buy that for a second. This is going to be a disaster." She smushed her lunch bag into a ball and stood up. "I've got to hit the office. See you."

The office, Lina thought. *Ramona works in the office. There's got to be a way to use that. But how?*

"Hey, Lina." Sebastiano had a prime seat on the front bleacher at the softball field, right behind the home bench. Lina sat down next to him. "What's happening? I logged onto the Dating Game and there was this Big Brother-ish note from Rod saying the school site would no longer carry it. What did you do to piss him off?"

"Nothing," Lina said. "Some parents complained and he shut us down. Too sexy."

"Hello, that's the whole point," Sebastiano said. "I wouldn't bother with it otherwise."

"We're going to get it back," Lina said. "Somehow." She had a glimmer of an idea, but it was so risky she didn't want to tell Sebastiano about it. It involved Ramona, and Lina would only share it on a need-to-know basis. That meant Holly and Mads—not Sebastiano. "What's the score?"

Spring Sports Saturday had arrived. Lina had just watched the boys' varsity lacrosse blow a lead and lose to archrival Draper. The game had gone into overtime, and Lina had missed half of the tennis tournament. She couldn't remember if she or Walker was supposed to cover tennis, anyway. But she knew he was doing girls' softball.

"It's 3-3 in the sixth," Sebastiano said. "We've got the winning run at the plate right now."

Lina checked out the RSAGE batter at the plate, who was knocking dirt out of her cleats and getting ready for the pitch. The visitor's pitcher threw a strike.

"I didn't know you were a softball fan," Lina said to Sebastiano.

"I'm not," Sebastiano said. "I'm scouting a Draper player for Holly. Apparently some Rosewood guy X-Rated her highly, and Holly wanted me to check her out." Holly was spending the day dress shopping with Julia. "Of course, now that there's no Dating Game, it doesn't make much difference."

"Holly has a hard time turning off her matchmaking instinct," Lina said. "Which girl are you scouting?"

"Right field. Hard to see her from here," Sebastiano said. "My first impression is she's a hot-tempered spitfire type."

"Is that good or bad?" Lina asked.

"Depends," Sebastiano said.

"Have you see Walker?"

"Right in front of you." Sebastiano pointed to the players' bench just six feet away. Walker was sitting with his back to them in deep discussion with Flynn.

"Here comes the pitch," Sebastiano said. "And—strike two!"

Lina watched Walker. His head was turned toward Flynn, away from the game. He hadn't even seen that pitch! How could he write a decent story on the game if he wasn't even watching?

"Full count," Sebastiano said. "Here comes the crucial pitch . . . and—ball four! No—the ump calls a strike!"

The batter and the umpire began to argue over the controversial pitch. Lina fumed. Walker hadn't even seen it! She got up and marched over to him. "Walker!" she snapped.

He looked up from his conversation with Flynn. "Hey, Lina."

"Are you covering this game?" Lina asked.

"Uh-huh. Shouldn't you be watching the tennis tournament?"

"I wasn't sure," Lina said. "That's what I came to ask you. But you're not even paying attention. You missed the last at bat—and it was the most crucial one of the game."

Walker's eyes trailed over to home plate, where the batter was kicking dirt on the umpire's shoes. "Bad call," he said. "I've got it covered."

"How do you know it's a bad call?" Lina asked. "You didn't see the pitch."

"Flynn, you're up," the softball coach called.

"Good luck," Walker said. Flynn leaned close to him, and he gave her a little kiss. Then she picked up her bat and bounced over to home plate. That little kiss made Lina's blood boil. So much for cool and professional. She felt ornery and spoiling for a fight.

"You shouldn't fraternize with the athletes while you're covering a game," Lina said, hating the snippy sound of her voice even as the words escaped her.

Walker stared at her. "I'm not fraternizing. I'm getting the inside dope."

She didn't really care how Walker covered the softball

game. She just wished he wouldn't be so into Flynn that he stopped paying attention. That wasn't like him. It wasn't the Walker she knew. The Walker she knew was the best reporter at the paper.

"What are you going to do, tell on me?" Walker said. "Go ahead. It's not like I'm getting paid or anything. What do you think Kate will do, fire me?"

"I don't care," Lina said. "I don't care what happens." She stormed away. She sensed someone running after her. She was afraid to look back, but she hoped—maybe it was Walker. Maybe he wanted to apologize.

"Lina!" It was Sebastiano. "Talk about hot-tempered spitfires. Not that it's any of my business, but I have to butt in—what was that little tiff about?"

"Nothing," Lina said.

"It didn't look like nothing to me," Sebastiano said. "Looked like a little lovers spat. Is there something going on I don't know about?"

"No," Lina said. "It was a sports argument. We're friends." *And that's all,* she thought as she trudged off to the tennis courts. She wished she didn't have to cover the tournament. She would rather have gone home, gone to bed, and pulled the covers over her head.

9 A Member of the Clan

To: hollygolitely
From: your daily horoscope

HERE IS TODAY'S HOROSCOPE: CAPRICORN: Don't try to do too much today. (For anyone else it would be a normal workload, but for you . . . 'nuff said.)

A few parents complain, and the principal completely shuts us down." Holly was explaining the problem to Julia, who had brought Holly to the cake designer for a tasting. But Holly wasn't in a tasting mood—she couldn't get the Dating Game off her mind. "Did you have Alvarado when you were at Rosewood?"

"Holly, focus," Julia said. "You're not tasting!" She

popped a piece of chocolate cake into Holly's mouth. Holly swallowed.

"That's good," Holly said. She speared another morsel of chocolate-iced chocolate cake and quickly ate it. "Chocolate is always good. So, anyway, my friends and I are trying to think of some way to get our blog back on the school site—"

"Did you try the strawberry cake?" Julia asked.

Holly had tried the strawberry. "It's not bad. But everybody loves chocolate. How can you go wrong?"

"There must be some people who don't like it, or all cakes would be chocolate," Julia said, licking the icing off her lips. There were so many options: carrot, vanilla, red velvet, strawberry . . . But taste-wise, chocolate won hands down.

"You can have a chocolate cake base," the designer, a small, neat woman named Carmen, said. "But if you want chocolate icing, that means a brown wedding cake. Most brides aren't into that."

"What do you think, Holly?" Julia asked.

"I see what she means," Holly said. "Brown isn't very bridal. And you don't want to get chocolate stains on your wedding dress when Michael smushes cake into your face."

"He won't do that," Julia said. "I forbid it."

"That might not stop him," Holly said. "It wouldn't stop Rob. But you know Michael and I don't, so—"

Julia ate another chocolaty bite. "Mmmm . . . But it's so good. Even if the cake were brown, wouldn't my guests thank me for sending them to choco-nirvana?"

"What about your dream scheme?" Holly reached into her bag and pulled out a colorful page torn from a magazine. It showed a five-tiered yellow cake trimmed in pale pink and green roses. "Remember the pink-and-green retro-seventies palette?"

That morning Julia had said that she saw a pink-and-green Lily Pulitzer-style preppy wedding in a dream and that that was what she wanted. On the other hand, two days earlier she'd wanted Tiffany blue and silver. Holly was beginning to notice that Julia changed her mind a lot.

Carmen looked at the picture. "With a cake like that, I'd do lemon or vanilla."

"Lemon!" Julia sighed. "That sounds so refreshing. Summery. And I wasn't going to let it sway me, but before I left the house, Mom said, 'Whatever you do don't pick chocolate.' I forget why. I think her whole side of the family is allergic to it or something.'"

Julia had originally planned on bringing Mrs. Safran cake tasting and dress shopping with her, but when Mrs. Safran's daily migraine arrived, Holly was called in to sub.

Holly didn't really mind, but she was looking forward to the arrival of Julia's friends from Boston next week. Maybe they could take over some of the wedding duties. They were Julia's bridesmaids, after all.

"I need your decision this week," Carmen reminded them. "If you want the cake in time for the wedding."

"I like peppermint a lot, too," Julia said. "Do you make peppermint cakes?"

"I'd suggest mint ice cream," Carmen said. "Not with lemon, though."

"I don't know what to do," Julia said. "I wish I could have five different cakes."

"That's always an option," Carmen said. "But it would probably run you close to—"

"Julia, you can't have five cakes," Holly said. "Just pick one—it's no big deal."

"I can't," Julia said. "Look—it's almost six. Do you want to come over for dinner tonight?"

Holly looked at Carmen, who seemed annoyed. She bustled about, getting ready to close her shop. "We'll have to get back to you about the cake," Holly said.

"All right, but do it soon," Carmen said.

Holly and Julia gathered up their shopping bags and got into Holly's yellow VW Beetle. "You were no help," Julia said.

"What do you mean?" Holly asked. "You want me to choose your cake for you? How hard is it to pick a cake?"

"You're right," Julia said. "I just get overwhelmed. We made so many choices already today—"

Actually, Holly thought, that wasn't true. Julia looked at wedding dresses in four different shops but couldn't narrow it down to fewer than six. She asked Holly which dresses she liked best for the rehearsal dinner; Holly chose her three favorites, and Julia bought them all, unable to decide.

Holly pulled up at the Safrans' house. "I probably shouldn't stay for dinner," she said. "I've got a history test to study for, and this big history project to work on that I've barely started, and then there's the blog. We can't just let it die!"

She wanted to see Rob, but at the Safrans' house there wasn't much point. They were hardly ever alone there.

"Oh, blog schmog," Julia said. "If you don't come in you'll hurt Rob's feelings. I wonder what Gabe's making tonight?"

Gabe had taken over most of the cooking since Mrs. Safran didn't feel much like doing it. Rob helped him sometimes. Their specialty was pasta.

Holly and Julia walked in, their arms full of shopping bags. The kitchen windows were steamy, and Rob and

Gabe stood at the island chopping onions. Actually, Gabe was chopping them and Rob was juggling them.

"How'd you do, girls?" Gabe asked. "How many credit cards did you max out today?"

Holly put down her bags, and Rob tossed her an onion. She caught it and tossed it back. "Stay for dinner, Holls?" Rob asked. "We're making Spaghetti ala Gabe."

"Smells good," Holly said. "What's in it?"

"Turkey meatballs," Gabe said

Rob pulled her close and breathed into her ear: "Please? Maybe we can escape later."

Her pulse quickened. "Okay, I'll stay," Holly said.

He kissed her ear to show her he was glad. Then he rubbed his nose in her hair. "Mmm, you smell better than the spaghetti sauce."

"Break it up, you two. Where's Mom?" Julia asked.

"Resting," Gabe said.

"Come on, Holly. Help me bring the bags into my room."

Holly broke away from Rob and followed Julia into her room, dropping the bags on the bed. "Call me when dinner's ready," Julia said. "I'm going to take a shower."

Holly returned to the kitchen. She felt so at home there that she set the table without having to ask where anything was.

"A little vino?" Gabe asked, pouring red wine into each of four glasses. "After all, it's Saturday night."

"Want to catch a movie later?" Rob asked Holly.

Holly hesitated. She was jonesing for a make-out session with Rob, and a movie would be perfect. But . . . "I really should study for my history test. I guess I can cram tomorrow. And Lina and Mads and I promised each other we'd come up with five ways to save the Dating Game by Monday, or it's finished forever! And we can't let that happen, not after we've worked so hard on it . . . plus on top of all that I've got this giant history project. . . ."

"You mean Cantwell's modern world history extravaganza?" Rob asked. "The end-of-semester blowout that counts for fifty percent of your grade?"

"That's the one," Holly said. "It's due in a couple of weeks and I don't even know what my topic is. What did you do for yours last year?"

"Built a diorama," Rob said.

Gabe snorted. "A diorama? How lame can you get?"

"Hey, man, it was the mother of all dioramas," Rob said. "It was practically the size of this kitchen island. It showed the city of Paris during the French Revolution, from the palace to the senate to the barricades in the streets. I even made a working guillotine where I could cut my little doll peoples' heads off—and red food coloring leaked out for blood."

"Cool," Holly said.

"I got an A," Rob said. "But it took weeks of work. You better get started, Holls."

"Did you have Cantwell for history, Gabe?" Holly asked.

"Yup. I didn't get an A, though."

"What did you do?"

"I tried to show the birth of the trade unions after the Triangle Shirtwaist Company's fire," Gabe said. "So I basically drew some windows on a shoebox and set it on fire. Cantwell said it didn't show much thought or research."

"Talk about lame," Rob said.

"I know. I got a D. I sucked at history."

Holly's phone buzzed. She glanced at it. Mads was texting her.

Lina had brilliant idea. Ramona—rod's office—ax-s codes!

What? Holly texted back.

We can hack on2 schl site! Call me ltr.

"Everything cool?" Rob asked.

"Very," Holly said. "Looks like we found a way to fight back. Against Rod, I mean."

"Is dinner ready yet?" Julia walked in wearing a bathrobe and drying her hair with a towel.

"Almost." Gabe gave the tomato sauce a stir and glanced at Julia. "But I require proper attire at my restaurant. Jeez, Julia, at least put some jeans on. You're as bad as Mom."

"All right, all right." Julia left. Gabe shook his head and clucked maternally. "I don't know what's gotten into that girl."

A few minutes later, Gabe was tossing the pasta in the sauce while Rob mixed the salad. Julia came in, dressed in sweats, plopped down next to Holly, and handed her a sheet of paper.

"What's this?" Holly asked.

"It's a list of things I need you to do for me tomorrow," Julia said.

Holly looked at it.

1. Call photographer and confirm booking.
2. Pick up summer dresses from cleaners.
3. Call salon—make hair, makeup, and manicure appointments for day before ceremony. . . .

The list went on. Holly stared at Julia in disbelief.

This was the bulk of the wedding work. "Um, shouldn't *you* be doing all this stuff?"

"What do you mean?"

"Well, you're the bride," Holly said. "I'm just the bride's brother's girlfriend. I don't mind giving you my opinion on a few details, but—"

"I'm doing a lot of work, too," Julia said. "But it's so hard to do it alone, and Mom's no help. Please, please, Holly. I really need you. You're so good at this stuff, and I'm such a space case. And this way you get to spend time with Rob."

Rob had only been half-listening, but he turned from the counter at the sound of his name and waved.

"Like you said, you're his girlfriend," Julia said. "You're part of the family. And everyone in the family pitches in to help, right?"

"What about your mother?" Holly couldn't help pointing this out.

"Except Mom," Julia said. "Special circs."

"But Julia, I've got to start my history project tomorrow. It's half my grade—"

"You've got plenty of time for that," Julia said. "Besides, those little errands won't take long."

Holly looked at the list again. Gather menus from five different caterers? She didn't even know how to do most of these things. And even if she did, it would take a week to finish everything on the list.

Julia leaned close, took Holly's hand in hers, and said softly, so that the boys didn't hear, "I can't tell you how much it means to me. And Rob and Gabe. And Mom. They may not say anything, but this is such a hard time for us, and having you around, an extra pair of hands . . ." Her eyes teared up. She wiped them with her napkin. "You're so sweet. Really. Sometimes I think if it weren't for you, this whole family would be falling apart."

"I don't want your family to fall apart—"

"I know you don't," Julia said. "Because you're a good person. A beautiful person with a generous heart."

"Well, I don't know about that—"

"You are," Julia said. "So—you will help me, won't you? Promise?"

What could she say? "Yes. Of course I'll help you."

"Promise?"

"Promise."

"Dinner is served!" Gabe called, carrying loaded plates to the table. Holly folded up the list and put it in her pocket. She couldn't help feeling annoyed with Julia. It was *her* wedding, not Holly's. Holly wanted to help, but she didn't want to do *everything*. Julia was trying to make her feel guilty about it, as if helping her were Holly's duty or something. Holly was beginning to see Rob's sister in a new light. She sure was good at getting her way.

Rob set the salad on the table, sat down on Holly's other side, and gave her a kiss. "Great to have you here, Holls."

Julia lifted her glass of wine. "A toast. To Holly—practically a member of the clan."

10 Going Underground

To:	mad4u
From:	your daily horoscope

HERE IS TODAY'S HOROSCOPE: VIRGO: You're getting so bold! You'll pay for it, but it's nice to see someone really put herself out there.

"Lina! Did you get the code?" Mads asked.

"Got it," Lina said. She gave Mads a slip of paper. "But I feel funny about this."

Mads, Lina, and Holly huddled in Holly's bedroom Sunday for an emergency blog meeting. When Lina told her that Ramona had access codes and could write on the school Web site, Mads knew she was onto something. She wanted to get started right away.

"Why do you feel funny? The moral high ground is totally on our side," Mads said. "We're being censored! Denied our rights as American citizens, just because we're in high school. Doesn't that piss you off?"

"Sure, it does," Lina said. "But we're also blatantly disobeying the principal. We could get into a lot of trouble."

"It's pretty serious, Mads," Holly said. "I'm with you all the way, but we should realize we're taking a risk."

"It's not that risky," Mads said. "We'll hide the blog where no one will ever find it—unless they know where to look."

That was the plan: to plant the Dating Game back on the school site, hidden at the end of the summer reading list. The only problem was that they needed a teacher-access code in order to write on that part of the site. Ramona worked in the school office and had access to the codes. She was more than happy to pass on the code in the name of subversive activity. She loved anything secret and dangerous.

Using the access code, Holly sat at her computer and transferred the Dating Game, X-Ratings, questionnaires, and all, to the end of the summer reading list.

"All we have to do is spread the word so people can find it," Mads said. "But only the right people. Students, not parents."

"That's what scares me," Lina said. "What if this leaks out somehow? What if somebody tells on us?"

"Anyone who does that will face a firing squad," Mads said. "Just kidding."

"Finished," Holly said, turning away from her screen. "The Dating Game is back in business."

"You know what?" Mads' mind was humming. "Maybe it wouldn't be so bad if this leaked. There is serious injustice here. We shouldn't be hiding it—we should draw attention to it. That's the only way we'll really beat this for good."

"How could we get more attention?" Holly said. "The school paper has covered the story."

"The school paper is small-time," Mads said. "We need something bigger."

"But why would anyone outside of the school care about our little blog?" Lina asked.

"National Radio Network cared about it," Mads said.

Holly's phone rang. "Hello?" she said. "Oh hi, Julia."

"She called twice before you got here," Mads whispered to Lina.

"What does she want?" Lina asked.

"First she asked if Holly thought she should wear flowers in her hair or a veil," Mads said. "Holly said flowers, and ten minutes later Julia called back and said, 'What kind of flowers?'"

"Julia, if you want to wear a veil, wear a veil," Holly said. "You're the bride. You can do whatever you want. Uh-huh. Uh-huh. Well, Rob was going to come over here that night. . . . No, don't put her on. . . . Hi, Mrs. Safran."

Mads looked at Lina. Now what was going on? Holly covered her eyes with her hands as if she had a headache. All along, in the back of her mind, Mads was still thinking about the Dating Game, turning over ideas.

"I'm sorry you're not feeling well," Holly said. "I understand. Sure. I'd be glad to help Julia address the invitations. Three hundred people is an awful lot. Okay. I'll be over later. Hope you feel better." After a pause she said, "Julia? When are your bridesmaids coming? You know, your bridesmaids? Deirdre and Bethany? Aren't they flying in from Boston soon to help you? Oh. They had to postpone it? Not until then? All right. Just wondering. Okay. See you in a couple hours." She hung up.

"What was that all about?" Mads asked.

"Julia's kind of overwhelmed by the wedding," Holly said. "Her mother's not into it, and I think Julia feels like she's doing everything alone."

"So she ropes you into helping her," Lina said.

"Well, I'm around a lot, seeing Rob," Holly said. "Or trying to, anyway. We can't get a minute alone lately. We haven't had a good solid make-out session in a week!"

"Bummer," Mads said. "At least you get to see your boyfriend. Stephen's always busy with some project, or away somewhere." She glanced at Lina, who was the worst off of all. Lina told her and Holly about Walker and Flynn right after her fight with Walker, when she was still fuming. Mads was shocked. She just didn't see it. But Lina's anger had faded into sadness.

"Did you read Walker's piece in *The Seer* this week?" Lina asked. "'Varsity Swimmers Drown Draper'? He's so good with words."

The Seer. That made Mads start thinking about the blog again, and censorship, and press coverage . . .

"'Drown Draper.' That's cute," Holly said, humoring Lina. "Let me fix you up with somebody else. Please! It will help you forget about Walker."

"That's impossible," Lina said. "And, anyway, with my luck, here's what will happen: You'll fix me up with some dork, and I won't like him because I'm hung up on Walker, but then finally I'll get over Walker and start liking the dork. But my heart will break because by then, he'll have another girlfriend. You see, it's hopeless. Life is just a big circle of unrequited love. Mads isn't listening."

"I am, too," Mads said, but she was really only half-listening. She had an idea, but it had nothing to do with Walker.

"I know how we can get lots of attention," she said. "A strike!"

"What are you talking about?" Holly asked.

"To protest the censorship at school," Mads said. "We'll have a huge rally. A full-school strike. A walkout! Rosewood has over eight hundred students. If everyone walks out of school at once, people will notice. I'll bet we can get the local news to cover it."

"But how will we get everyone in school to strike at once?" Holly asked.

"E-mail," Mads said. "I'll send out a mass e-mail to everyone in school. And you guys spread the word at school. We tell everybody to tell everybody. We can make flyers, too, and stuff them in people's lockers. At two o'clock Friday afternoon, everybody in school—I mean *everybody*—will drop whatever he or she is doing and walk out."

"Right in the middle of class?" Lina asked.

"Exactly," Mads said. "Teachers can't ignore this. Rod can't ignore it. The whole student body will show our solidarity. What do you think?"

"It's daring," Holly said.

"We could get into *big* trouble for this," Lina said. "Mads, I don't think we should do it. Rod will suspend us for sure. If we call a strike . . . my parents will kill me."

"I don't want a suspension on my record," Holly said.

"I don't want to be suspended, either," Mads said. "But I can't sit by and let Rod and the parents get away with this. I just can't! Look, it's my idea. I'm going to do it no matter what. If we get into trouble, I'll take the blame."

"Mads, no," Lina said. "We'll stick with you."

"I'm not worried," Mads said. "What are they going to do—suspend the whole school?"

STUDENT STRIKE!!!!!

Fight censorship! Support the Dating Game! We are calling for a school-wide student strike on Friday afternoon at two o'clock. When the sixth-period bell rings, drop what you're doing and walk quietly and calmly to the front lawn of the school. You will then receive further instructions.

IMPORTANT: For this to work, we need total, 100% participation! No wimpouts! College wonks worried about your transcripts—wake up! A good college will respect you for standing up for civil rights and working for free speech and equality, etc. Call it an extracurricular activity. And, anyway, if you don't join us, you're a weenie and no college will take you, anyway. Bonus: You'll be on TV! Channel 7 News promised to be there to cover the story. Plus, you'll miss 45 minutes of class! How can you lose? Spread the word!

11 Elvira

To:	linaonme
From:	your daily horoscope

HERE IS TODAY'S HOROSCOPE: CANCER: In the movies, great couples overcome obstacles and misunderstandings before they get together. In real life, they just have problems.

Your name: *Elvira Webber*

Your grade: *10th*

Your ex's name: *Walker Moore*

Your ex's grade: *11th*

How do you know him/her? *school*

How long were you together? *Too long*

Who dumped who? *I dumped him—you think I'm some kind of idiot?*

Why did you break up? *Where do I start? Basically, he's a jerk.*

Are you friends now? *I don't make friends with jerks.*

What do you think of your ex as a friend? *See above*

What do you think of your ex as a boyfriend/girlfriend? (What was good and bad about him or her? Vices? Habits? Hang-ups? Family problems?) *He's a player. He cheated on me more than once—that I know of. He's totally selfish. Sure, he seems sweet on the surface, but trust me—that's an act. And I find it scary that a person can fool so many people. . . . There are tons of little things wrong with him, too. If I had to name just one, it would be—rampant backne. Ick!*

What would a new person have to have (that you didn't have) to make a relationship with your ex work? *She'd have to be crazy. I'm not kidding. But I know what kind of girl he likes: the kind of nervous, snooty girl who can't resist mentioning the fact that she has famous Hollywood-director relatives. Just shows what sort of person he is—he pretends to be cool, but deep down, he's a social climber.*

On a scale of 1 to 10, with 10 being the highest, you rate your ex: *negative 10 billion*

"Jeez Louise," Lina said when she read Elvira's X-Rating. "How did this get on the site?"

It appeared on the Dating Game sometime during the night. Lina checked the blog that morning before school, and there it was. She didn't post it, she knew that much. And she couldn't believe Holly or Mads would have such bad judgment. It was so mean! But how else could it have gotten there? She had to talk to them right away.

"Yikes, that is mean," Mads said. "I'd never post it without talking to you first, Lina. Especially since it's about Walker."

"I haven't posted any X-Ratings all week," Holly said.

Lina had dragged them into the library to check out the site as soon as she got to school. "I don't get it," she said. "If none of us posted it, how did it get there?"

The mystery preoccupied Lina at school all morning. Was this the same Walker Lina knew? Could any of this be true? Or was it just a joke—a very mean joke? Sure, she was annoyed with Walker, but she didn't think he deserved anything like this.

"What is that supposed to be?" Sebastiano asked her later on in art class. "A plane crash?"

Lina was trying to make a birthday card for her father. Next to her, Mads, who was better at art, was taking headshots of people in her family and putting them on top of animal bodies.

"It's not supposed to be anything," Lina said. "It's abstract. For my father's birthday."

"I guess your father has pretty gory taste," Sebastiano

said. "Use a little more blood-red, why don't you. That doesn't say, 'Happy Birthday.' It says, 'I know what you did last summer.'"

Lina looked at her collage and realized he was right. It was way too red. She grabbed some slips of blue paper and started pasting over it.

"And Mads, why are you putting your sister's head on the body of a cockroach?" Sebastiano asked.

"Art is an expression of truth," Mads said. "You're so nosy, what are you making?"

"A 3-D collage in the shape of a disco ball," Sebastiano said. He showed them a half-finished sphere covered in pictures cut out from magazines. "Instead of mirrors, I'm covering it with pictures of everybody on *Desperate Housewives.*"

"Very ambitious," Lina said. Sebastiano sat down at the next table and started flipping through old issues of *People,* scissors in hand.

"I can't stop thinking about Elvira," Lina said to Mads. "It has to be a joke. A made-up name. But who would do that? And why? What does she have against Walker?"

"It's weird," Mads said. "Walker's popular. Everybody likes him."

"I know," Lina said. "Could somebody be out to get him?"

"Or did he really mistreat some girl who couldn't wait to blow his nice-guy cover?" Mads said.

"It's not a cover," Lina said. "He really is nice."

"And what about Flynn?" Mads said. "That description of the kind of girl Walker likes was obviously Flynn. I'm not crazy about her, but that was pretty mean. But even if someone's out to get Walker, why go after Flynn, too?"

"It has to be someone who has access to the site," Lina said. "But we're the only ones. Except for Rod, of course, and his secretary—"

"—and Ramona," Mads said. "She has the access code. Duh. That's where we got it from in the first place."

"And she was with me when we heard Flynn talking about Walker," Lina said. "She knows how hurt I was. And she hates Flynn on principal. She'd have no problem doing something mean to her."

"And if it screws up your life and hurts Walker, too, what does she care?" Mads said. "She likes causing trouble."

"And eavesdropping," Lina added with an eye on Sebastiano. "Are you listening to us?" she asked him.

"No," he said. "I'm incapable of cutting out pictures of celebrities and listening to you talk at the same time. It takes too much coordination." He snapped his scissors at her. "Of course, I'm eavesdropping! You want my advice?"

"No," Lina and Mads said at once.

"Don't jump to conclusions," Sebastiano said.

"That's terrible advice," Mads said.

"We didn't jump to conclusions. We figured it out logically," Lina said. "It had to be Ramona."

After lunch, Lina realized she'd left her father's birthday card in the art studio. She went upstairs to the third floor to get it. As she approached the room, she heard voices—mainly a shrill girl's voice, yelling.

"Just tell me if it's true!" the girl shouted. *That's Flynn*, Lina realized. "Are you really a player? Are you cheating on me right now?"

"No, Flynn, I swear!" Walker said. "That whole thing is a giant pack of lies."

Lina hid in the hallway and listened.

"Who is Elvira, anyway?" Flynn cried. "Such a stupid name. How could you ever go out with a girl named Elvira?"

"I've never heard of her, Flynn," Walker said. "I have no idea who she is."

"You're lying!" Flynn said. "Just like Elvira said. You're lying to protect your old girlfriend. Maybe you still like her! You probably like her even more because she insulted me!"

"Insulted you? What are you talking about?"

"Didn't you notice how she dissed me?" Flynn said. "It wasn't very subtle. She's jealous because I have an aunt in the film business."

"Oh, that."

"Yes, that! Don't you care? You don't care that some ex-girlfriend of yours humiliated me in front of the whole school? Don't you have any loyalty to me at all?"

"Of course I do, Flynn." Walker's voice was pleading. Lina felt sorry for him. "I'm telling you, I don't know any Elvira. She's no ex of mine. She made all that stuff up. Why won't you believe me?"

"I want to believe you," Flynn said. "It's just so shocking. . . . Lift up your shirt."

"What?"

"I want to see if you have backne."

"Flynn, trust me, I don't have backne."

"Lift up your shirt!"

"No."

"You do have backne, don't you!"

There was a struggle, and Lina peeked and saw Flynn trying to lift up Walker's shirt and Walker struggling to hold it down.

"Flynn, I'm telling you, I don't—"

"Just show me! What's your problem?"

"Stop it! Please believe me," Walker said. He held Flynn's hands. She let go of his shirt.

"If you show me your back and you don't have backne, it will prove that she's lying," Flynn said.

"And if you take my word for it and don't strip me naked at school, it will prove that you trust me," Walker said.

"Are you going to show me your back or not?"

"This is ridiculous," Walker said. "No."

Lina pressed herself against the wall as Flynn ran out of the art room and down the stairs. Walker ran after her, calling her name. Luckily, the door to the art room hid Lina pretty well.

She heard their footsteps rattling down the stairs. Lina went into the art room and found her card. She sat down and rested her head on her arms. *Ramona, what have you done?*

"There you are." Walker's voice had a sharpness to it that Lina had never heard before. He marched up to her at a lacrosse game that afternoon, all business. "I've been looking for you all day. Have you been avoiding me? I don't blame you. I wouldn't want to get blasted the way I'm about to blast you, either."

Lina shrank down in her seat. "Walker, I understand—"

"You don't understand anything!" Walker shouted. "How could you do this to me, Lina? Why would you?"

"Walker, I didn't do anything, I swear," Lina said. "I read Elvira online just like you did. I think I know who posted it, but it wasn't me or Mads or Holly—"

"Whoever wrote that was trying to break up me and Flynn," Walker said. "Who else could it be?" He threw her an accusing stare.

"It wasn't me!" Lina was shaking. How could he think she'd do something so awful? Did he dislike her that much? "I'm not trying to break up anybody. I promise, I had nothing to do with it!"

"I don't believe you," Walker said. "You're responsible for the Dating Game. For the content that goes online. If you didn't like it, if you thought it would hurt someone, you could have stopped it. But you didn't. I think you wanted to hurt someone, Lina. Me."

Lina could hardly speak. Her heart was cracking like glass.

"If this is the sort of thing you run on your blog, I'm not sure I want to support it," Walker said. "Maybe Rod is right: the Dating Game should be shut down. It's destructive—a mean thing run by a mean girl who's using it for her own ends—to hurt people."

He turned around and walked away, leaving Lina pressing her fists to her chest, wishing the pain would stop.

12 Strike!

To:	mad4u
From:	your daily horoscope

HERE IS TODAY'S HOROSCOPE: VIRGO: You're in a very disruptive mood these days, which is fine if you're willing to take the consequences. However, you are not.

Mads fidgeted more than usual in geometry Friday afternoon. She stared at the minute hand of the clock on the wall. Two minutes to two. Soon the bell would ring. Everyone would get up—and then what? Would they all go to their next class like a bunch of sheep? Or would they follow her to the front of the building in a moving display of solidarity? Would she and Lina and Holly find themselves standing alone on the lawn, shrieking slogans through a megaphone, their words falling on deaf ears? Or would they be buoyed on a tide of goodwill and peaceful protest?

The minute hand ticked. Sixty seconds to go.

This will really show how popular the Dating Game is, Mads thought. *And how much power we can have. If it means anything to this school, the kids will show up. If not . . .*

Click. Two o'clock. The bell rang. Class over.

Mads got up out of her seat. Autumn Nelson smiled and nodded at her. So did Derek Scotto.

Mads left Ms. Weymouth's room and walked down the hall. A stream of people trailed her. More kids walked out of their classrooms and joined the march. Mads spotted Dan Shulman—the IHD teacher whose assignment had started this whole thing—leave his classroom and walk outside with the students. He nodded at Mads and gave her a little fist-pump in solidarity.

Mads met Lina and Holly at the door to the school. They went outside and positioned themselves on the front steps. Mads reached behind a bush where she had stashed a megaphone borrowed from the gym equipment room.

"Wow, Mads," Lina said. "Look at this!"

Students were pouring out of the school building. Some teachers followed and hovered around the edges of the crowd. Some of them looked confused, while others frantically tried to herd their students back inside the building. No one paid attention to them. Dan was encouraging the students to protest as they walked past him.

"It worked," Mads said in amazement. "The whole school is going along with this!"

When the building was empty, Mads lifted her megaphone and shouted, "All right, Rosewood! Thank you for coming! You're my heroes!"

The crowd cheered. It was a warm, sunny afternoon and very pleasant to be outside instead of in class. A few kids were already lounging on the grass. Mads took a breath to calm her edgy nerves. She'd never spoken in front of so many people before. She passed the megaphone to Lina.

"Mr. Alvarado and a few parents are trying to control what we can write about ourselves!" Lina shouted. "Are we going to let them?"

"NO!" the crowd yelled.

"Down with censorship!" Holly cried. Mads, Lina, and the crowd picked up the chant. "Down with censorship! Down with censorship!"

A white Channel 7 News van pulled up in front of the school, and a cameraman and a reporter jumped out.

"Channel 7 is here!" Mads said, and the crowd cheered louder than ever. "Let's show them we mean business!"

The chant went up again. "Down with censorship!" The camera filmed the huge mob of students and then aimed at the reporter, who stood in front of the crowd.

The front doors of the school burst open, and Rod appeared with a megaphone of his own. "All right, you've had your fun," he yelled. "Enough is enough. Get back inside the building and return to your classes immediately!"

"Boo! Boo!" the kids jeered.

"Anyone who isn't back in school within five minutes is facing suspension!" Rod cried. "Inside! Inside!"

"Boo!"

Mads started a counter-chant. "Free speech for all!" The crowd took it up, clapping.

"Listen to me!" Rod shouted. "I agree with you! I am against censorship! I am for free speech!"

Mads was shocked. "Did he change his mind already? These protests really work fast."

The crowd jeered. They didn't believe him.

"So if you will all return to class, we can discuss it calmly," Rod said. "Everyone back inside!"

Rod waved his arms toward the school building. He was booed and shouted down so loudly, he dropped his megaphone and gave up. He went back inside the school to wait it out.

Dan and his girlfriend, French teacher Camille Barker, chanted along with the students. "We're not the only ones who believe in free expression!" Lina called into her microphone. "Some of the teachers are behind us, too!"

The rally went on for forty-five minutes with everyone, peacefully but forcefully chanting, singing, and shouting, until the bell for the next class rang. "That's it!" Mads shouted. "Thank you for coming! Our message has been heard loud and clear, thanks to you!"

She propped open the doors to the school, and the students began to file back inside. "That rocked!" kids told Mads, Lina, and Holly as they filed past. "Excellent!" "Can we do it again tomorrow?"

"I think once is enough for now," Mads said. "We sent Rod back inside with his tail between his legs. He saw that the whole school is on our side. Maybe by now he's ready to back down—at least a little."

"I hope so," Lina said.

"Everyone over to my house tonight after school," Holly said. "We've got to watch the six o'clock news!"

The mood in the halls was buoyant and happy as the students headed back to class. Mads was happiest of all.

"You just did something really big," Lina said. "Do you realize that?"

"Yeah," Mads said. "I do."

• • •

"Maybe we're not in trouble this time," Mads said. She was still high from the strike. She and Lina and Holly were sitting outside Rod's office at the end of the day, waiting to be called inside. "He said he was for free speech, remember? Maybe Rod just wants to tell us he surrenders."

"Are you crazy?" Holly said. "A principal doesn't call you into his office to tell you he surrenders."

"Sylvia is going to go ballistic," Lina said. Mads could see the panic on her face and felt terrible for her. "She does this Freeze-Queen thing where she doesn't talk to you or look at you but you know she's pissed, and you're just waiting for her to blow. . . . The suspense is the worst part. . . ."

The door to Rod's office opened, and he beckoned them inside. The girls went in and sat down. He leaned back in his chair, frowning at each girl in turn.

"I understand that you have disobeyed me and hidden your blog in a secret place on the school Web site," Rod said. "Is this true?"

"Yes." Mads shifted in her seat.

The girls nodded. There was no point in denying it.

"I know about it because I've received another complaint," Rod said. "Again about this X-Rating feature. Apparently a girl named Elvira wrote some very nasty things about some of our students."

Ramona! Mads thought. *Her stupid joke!*

"And then there is the strike you organized today," Rod said. "You completely disrupted school. That cannot be allowed."

He rubbed his large, shiny forehead. He looked pained. Mads felt sorry for him; she could tell that though he didn't like to be disobeyed, he disliked punishing people even more.

"Ladies, your brazenness astounds me," Rod said. "I have no choice but to suspend all three of you. Starting now. Go to your lockers, get your things, and leave the building immediately. I'll call your parents and inform them. I'm sure they will all be quite unhappy."

Heads hanging, Holly and Lina stood up and prepared to leave. But Mads said, "Mr. Alvarado, please don't suspend Holly and Lina. This isn't their fault. I'm responsible. Me and only me."

"Mads, no—" Holly said.

"Don't lie, you guys," Mads said. "I organized the strike. It was one hundred percent my idea."

"Is it true?" Rod asked.

"Technically, but—" Lina began.

"Just answer yes or no," Rod snapped. "Is what Madison says true?"

Mads gave them her pleading stare, hoping they would save themselves. Why should they suffer for her actions? And why should they all three be punished when one could take the fall for all?

After a long pause, Lina answered, "Yes."

"Yes," Holly said.

"I believe you," Rod said. "All right. Lina and Holly, you may return to class. Madison, I'm afraid you are suspended from school for two weeks. You are not allowed at school or on school property during that time. If you violate this, you will be expelled. Understand?"

Mads swallowed. Now that it was happening—suspension!—it sounded so serious and scary. *Oh god,* she thought, *my parents. The Dark Overlord might actually live up to his name for once.*

She blinked back tears. No way was she going to cry in front of Rod. But it hurt to be punished when you were used to being good. *You asked for it, you got it,* she said to herself. "I understand," she said to Rod.

"And if that blog appears anywhere on the school site again, you will be expelled," Rod added. "See you in two weeks."

Holly and Lina had tears in their eyes, too, as they all left the office. They walked Mads to her locker.

"Mads, what are you going to do?" Lina asked.

"I'm going to use my free time to make things right," Mads said. "I'm going to find a way to show Rod and the parents' board that they can't stop us from expressing ourselves. I will make them put the Dating Game back on our school site."

"We'll help you, Mads," Holly said. "Let's all think of ways to do it."

"It won't be easy," Lina said.

"I know," Mads said. "But I'll have two weeks with nothing else to do but figure it out."

13 In Like Flynn

To: linaonme
From: your daily horoscope

HERE IS TODAY'S HOROSCOPE: CANCER: If life was fair, you'd be better-looking.

"Hi, Flynn," Lina said. "Can I talk to you for a minute?"

"What about?" Flynn asked.

Flynn was in the school musical, so Lina knew she could find her at rehearsal after school. She was hoping to straighten out this whole Elvira thing. Maybe then at least Walker wouldn't hate her. And not-hating could lead to liking, which could lead to like-liking . . . that was the theory, anyway.

Lina looked at Flynn's friends, who seemed eager to hear her answer. "It's private."

Lina had already gone to Ramona and accused her of being Elvira, but Ramona had denied it. Nothing Lina said could make Ramona admit her guilt. She was so stubborn! And she seemed to be going out of her way to cause problems. But that was Ramona. Causing problems was her lifestyle.

Flynn got out of her seat and followed Lina to the back of the auditorium, where they could have some privacy.

"It's about that X-Rating," Lina said. "From Elvira. I just wanted to tell you that I had nothing to do with it. I have an idea who might be behind it, but no proof. Yet—"

"Why are you telling me this?" Flynn demanded.

"Because I know you and Walker had a fight about it, and I think it's silly to let something like this come between you—"

"You think it's silly? Silly to be upset because I just found out my boyfriend is a player? Because I was insulted in front of the whole school?"

"I'm trying to tell you that the Elvira thing was fake," Lina said. "Think about it. When has Walker ever acted like a player?"

"How would I know? We just started going out. But you've known him longer. He used to talk about you a lot.

Not so much lately." Flynn paused and stared Lina right in the face. "I still don't get it. Why would you bother telling me this . . . ? Wait! There's only one reason. *You* must be Elvira!"

"What? I am not," Lina said. "I just wanted to help—"

"Because you feel guilty?" Flynn said. "Or because your plan backfired and now Walker's mad at you instead of running into your arms?"

"Flynn, that's ridiculous."

"I always thought there was something weird between you two," Flynn said. "He always said you were 'friends.' But everybody knows guys and girls can't be friends—not really. You like Walker and you're trying to steal him from me! It's the only explanation!"

Flynn's voice had risen to a shriek. "Flynn, listen, you've got this all wrong—"

"I don't believe you," Flynn said. "Get away from me. I don't want to talk to you again."

She marched up the aisle back to her friends, who were staring at Lina as if she were a circus freak.

So much for Plan A, Lina thought as she slipped out of the auditorium. *What a snippy little pain in the butt she is! How can Walker like her?*

Elvira's right about one thing, she thought. *Walker has sucky taste in girls.*

14 Mads in Exile

To:	mad4u
From:	your daily horoscope

HERE IS TODAY'S HOROSCOPE: VIRGO: I know I said you were maturing, but now I take it back. If you keep regressing at this rate, you'll be back in diapers within a week.

"You're what?!?" M.C. shrieked.

Mads thought she'd better break the news of her suspension to her parents as soon as possible—before they had a chance to return Rod's call. It wasn't going well.

"My innocent little girl!" M.C. cried. "What kind of delinquent have you turned into?"

"Calm down, honey," Russell said. "It's not as if she

was suspended for smoking or cheating or anything like that."

M.C. was curled up on the couch, hugging a pillow. Her eyes were wet behind her red cat's-eye glasses. "I know," she said. "But—suspended! What does it mean?"

"It just means I can't go to school for two weeks," Mads said.

"But it's almost the end of the year!" M.C. said. "You won't be prepared for your final exams. And what about your permanent record?"

"Um, I guess it'll have a little smudge on it." Mads was hoping to play this down, but that never worked with M.C. She was high-strung. "Unless I can get the suspension revoked. And I can."

"You can?" her father said. "How can you do that?"

"There's a big parents' board meeting next week," Mads said. "I'm going to state my case in front of them and convince them that this suspension is wrong. They have no right to censor the students! And all I'm really being punished for is speaking out."

"And disrupting school," M.C. reminded her.

"Only for one period," Mads said.

Russell gave her a hug. "I hope you can get the suspension reversed. If you need any help, let me know. I'm proud of you for standing up for what you believe in."

"Don't tell her that!" M.C. cried. "You'll only encourage her."

"I also agree with your mother that getting suspended isn't good," Russell added.

"Hey, get in here!" Audrey cried from the den. "Mads is on TV!"

They ran into the den to catch the Rosewood strike on the six o'clock news.

"Look at you!" Russell said proudly. "A real old-fashioned radical! You're the head honcho of this whole production, aren't you?"

"It was all my idea," Mads said.

"That's why you're in trouble now," her mother reminded her.

"You look fat," Audrey said.

"Shut up!" Mads said.

"It's peaceful, well-organized," Russell said. "Mads, I think you were right to protest."

"Don't say that!" M.C. said. "What about her record? What about college?"

"I know your mother secretly agrees with me," Russell said.

"I do not!" M.C. said. "Don't speak for me."

"See, Mom? That's what we were protesting about," Mads said. "The right to speak for ourselves."

"Oh, honey," M.C. said. "What are you going to do with yourself for two weeks?"

"It won't be a vacation. You'll have to keep up with your schoolwork," Russell said.

"And we're going to punish you," M.C. said. "Somehow. Right, Russell?"

"I guess we have to," Russell said. "This is serious."

"I know how you can punish her," Audrey said. "Make her be my slave! She has to do whatever I tell her to."

"I have a better idea," Mads said. "For punishment, I have to find the lowlifes who are your real parents!" Audrey wasn't adopted—she was the spitting image of M.C.—but sometimes Mads couldn't believe she was related to her.

"We'll think of something," Russell said.

Monday, Mads' first real day of suspension. It dragged. Russell and M.C. had yet to think up a punishment, but Mads was convinced that the boredom of staying home all day was punishment enough.

The doorbell rang. Finally, something that passed for excitement. Mads glanced at the clock. It was after four—time for a Lina/Holly update. Her father wasn't home from work yet, and her mother the pet shrink was downstairs in her office with a patient, a cat who hated its owner. Audrey was at a friend's house. Mads went to the door expecting to find Lina or Holly. Instead, she found Sean.

Without thinking, she threw open the door, then immediately regretted it. She was still wearing her pajamas (why get dressed? She hadn't left the house all day, and they were comfy). And not just any pajamas—SpongeBob SquarePants footie pajamas.

Sean took her in, shocked at first, and then laughed.

"Oh my god!" Mads cried. "I'll be right back!" She tried to slam the door shut, but Sean caught it and pushed it open again.

"Wait, it's okay," he said. "You look cute. I'm a big SpongeBob fan." He cracked up. Mads wanted to die. What was he doing popping over and surprising her like this with no warning? She would have gone out and gotten a makeover if she'd known. Or at least gotten dressed.

What *was* he doing there, anyway?

"Can I come in?" Sean asked.

"Please let me change," Mads said.

"I'm only going to stay a minute," Sean said. Mads let him in.

"Do you want something to drink or anything?" she asked him.

"A Coke would be great," he said. He followed her into the kitchen.

"We don't have any Coke," Mads said. Her mother was a health freak. She opened the fridge and scanned its contents. "How about an Herbal Kick Carrot-Celery Cooler?"

"Uh, pass. Listen, kid—Madison—I heard about what happened. That Rod suspended you and everything. Everybody's talking about it. And I just wanted to tell you I think it sucks. Totally janky. That school is supposed to be cool—different, you know? Even my mom's on your side."

"Really?" Mads was surprised. His mother was one of those perfectly dressed, perfectly made up types with a super-neat house (Mads had been there for a party once). Mads would have taken her for an anti-Dating Gamer. She looked uptight. "That's nice."

"Yeah," Sean said. "I just wanted to tell you I think what you're doing is awesome. I mean, standing up for yourself, for students' rights and all that. I-I totally admire it."

Mads' jaw dropped open. She had to use her hand to slap it shut. Sean had come to her house to tell her he *admired* her? Was she dreaming? It had to be a dream. In a few minutes she'd wake up to find Audrey standing over her, laughing and saying, "You should have heard what you were saying in your sleep!"

Sean stood up. "So, anyway, I wanted to tell you that everyone at school is behind you, so don't give up. I loved that walkout, by the way. Missed a Spanish pop quiz, turned out."

"Oh. Good." Mads had finally found her voice, but not, apparently, her brain. Slowly it recovered from the shock of being an object of Sean's admiration. And not a moment too soon. Tired of waiting for some kind of response from her, he headed for the front door.

"Sean, wait," Mads said. "Thanks. That really means a lot to me. I'm in pretty big trouble, and it's nice to know it's worth something."

"It is."

"Listen," she said. "Will you help me? I want to stage a huge rally at the parents' board meeting next Thursday. Will you spread the word?"

"No problem."

"Thanks. Bye!" She watched him trip down the jagged stone steps that led to the street, jump into his Jeep, and zoom away. Who knew public service could be such a turn-on?

linaonme: mads—how's the life o'leisure?
mad4u: boring—until sean came over.
linaonme: ?????

mad4u: 2 say how much he admires me

linaonme: ?????

mad4u: for being miss anti-censorship

linaonme: ?????

mad4u: stop doing that

linaonme: sorry. it's just so non-sean

mad4u: I know, but it happened. Makes it all worthwhile. I'd turn down a nobel peace prize for a shot at sean. how was school 2day?

linaonme: bleh. Walker still pissed.

mad4u: did u tell him ramona is elvira?

linaonme: no. she still denies it. we need proof. Or a confession.

mad4u: I've got nothing but time. I'll beat it out of her.

Mads was annoyed with Ramona. She got the Dating Game into extra trouble with this Elvira stuff, but she still wouldn't admit her guilt? It was wrong. And it was making things harder on Lina.

We've got to get her to confess, Mads thought. *Maybe then Walker will forgive Lina, and they can at least be friends again. If that's possible.*

First, to set the trap. Mads e-mailed Ramona and asked if they could meet at Vineland the next afternoon, just to bring Mads up-to-date on what was going on in

English class. Mads really didn't care about English class, of course. She was on Elvira's trail.

"What did you really want to talk about?" Ramona asked Mads at Vineland the next afternoon. "I know it isn't English. You could give a crap about that."

Mads was taken aback. She hadn't expected Ramona to see through her so quickly. But it didn't matter. The important thing was she had her suspect in sight.

"Okay, you're right," Mads said. "I wanted to ask you a question . . . ELVIRA!"

She leaned close to Ramona and spat out the name Elvira as if she were saying "Boo!" Ramona didn't flinch.

"You've got the wrong girl," Ramona said. "I'm not Elvira."

"Oh, come on," Mads said. "It's just the kind of name you'd pick. And I know you wanted to get Walker and Lina together—"

"So do you," Ramona said. "Are you Elvira?"

"No," Mads said. "And neither is Holly."

"Well, neither am I," Ramona said.

"But you're the only person who could be," Mads said. "You work in the school office. You even wrote down an access code for me. You're the only person who could tap into the Dating Game without us knowing."

"That's not true," Ramona said. "Rod could have done it. Or Ms. Ellen." Ms. Ellen was Rod's secretary.

"But they didn't," Mads said. "Don't toy with me. I'm a tough rebel now. I'm a bad girl. I've been *suspended*."

"Big whoop. Sorry, but it doesn't make you any more intimidating than you ever were. And you were always about as intimidating as a baby bunny."

"Hey! That's not nice. Just confess, Ramona. To help Lina."

"I'd love to help Lina, but I'm telling you, I'm not Elvira," Ramona said. "If you're through interrogating me, I've got homework to do. I go to school." She stood up and added, "I'll let you pay for the coffee."

Mads watched her go in disbelief. How could Ramona sit there and lie to her face that way? Repeatedly? Without blinking an eye? What kind of person does that? She'd never really been friends with Ramona—Ramona was more Lina's friend, and even Lina had mixed feelings about her.

Sorry, Lina, Mads thought. *I gave it my best shot. Ramona is too tough for me.*

15 The Bride Who Wouldn't Die

To:	hollygolitely
From:	your daily horoscope

HERE IS TODAY'S HOROSCOPE: CAPRICORN: What happened to you? You used to be cool.

When her phone buzzed on Saturday, Holly tried to ignore it. She'd spent the morning e-mailing couples she'd matched, asking for their support in saving the Dating Game. She gathered any success stories she found and even tried to find benefits in the relationships that hadn't worked out.

Then she went to the library that morning to do research for her history project. She'd finally decided on a topic: the Russian Revolution. She planned to write a diary from the point of view of Anastasia, one of the doomed daughters of the czar. She wanted to get a lot done that morning because Mo Basri was having a big pool party that afternoon. It was two-thirty—almost time to head for the party.

The buzzing stopped, then started again. Holly had gathered a big pile of books and was engrossed in the story of Rasputin, the monk who had the Russian royal family under his spell. Rasputin's enemies did everything they could to kill him—they drugged him, poisoned him, and even beat and shot him. He survived it all. Then, when they gave up and simply dumped him into the river, he drowned. *Maybe I should do my project on Rasputin instead,* Holly thought. *I could call it, "The Monk Who Wouldn't Die."*

The phone buzzed a third time. She couldn't resist glancing at it to see who was calling, even though she knew: Julia. And she was right. Julia: The Bride Who Wouldn't Stop Calling.

Holly knew she'd get no peace until she answered the call, so she might as well get it over with. "Hello?"

"Holly, where are you?" Julia asked. "You're supposed to meet Deirdre and Bethany at the dressmakers for their fittings at three."

"They're here? Finally," Holly said. No maybe she'd

be free. Julia could wrangle them into helping her with all her decisions.

"Do you really need me?" Holly asked. "Can't they get fitted themselves?"

"Yes, but you're supposed to help them pick out the fabric for their dresses, remember?" Holly didn't remember this, but she'd been so busy lately she could have spaced it. Apparently Deirdre and Bethany were as helpless in making decisions as Julia was. Or at least Julia thought they were.

"I can't." By three, Holly planned on being poolside at Mo's with her friends, including Rob.

"And while you're there, show them the material we picked out and make sure they choose a good color, nothing hideous," Julia added.

"Julia, didn't you hear me? I can't go," Holly said.

"Why not?"

"I'm working on a school project," Holly said. "And the blog. And then there's this pool party—"

"A party! Holly, this is way more important than a party. Besides, it will only take a few minutes."

That was what Julia always said.

"You have no idea what a hard time I'm having finding a justice of the peace," Julia said. "And a good gardening service to clean up the yard. And dealing with Mom.

You promised to help me. I'm your boyfriend's sister."

"Rob's going to be at the party," Holly said.

"You can go, too," Julia said. "Just stop by Melissa's on the way." Melissa's was the dress shop.

"Please, Julia—they're your friends. Don't you trust them to pick out a dress in a decent color?"

"No," Julia said. "They're both morons. I need you there, Blondie." Holly could hear her tearing up over the phone. "I'm so overwhelmed with all of these things to do, and the whole idea of getting *married*, and Dad and Mom splitting up and everything . . . What? Oh hi, Mom. Want to say hello to Holly?"

"No! Don't put her on. I've got to go," Holly said.

"You'll stop at Melissa's?" Julia said.

"Yes, I'll stop by, just for a minute," Holly said, thinking, *Why, why do I fall for this same line every time?* Because it was beginning to feel like a line to her. Like manipulation. But Holly could see Julia's trouble. She had gotten in way over her head, trying to plan this wedding all alone in six weeks. And there were a lot of emotions bouncing off the walls at the Safran house, not that you'd know it from Rob, but still.

Maybe the dressmaker wouldn't take too long. Maybe she'd have time to stop by Mo's pool party before it was over, and at least get her feet wet.

"Thank you, Holly. You have no idea how much this means to me. You're a lifesaver! Bye!"

Holly sighed and closed her Russian history book. So much for research.

"I still don't understand why you couldn't go to Mo's," Lina said. She had met Holly outside her locker Monday morning.

"I told you, those girls are psychopaths," Holly said. "Deirdre kept insisting that the dressmaker took her measurements wrong, that her waist couldn't be that big. And when I showed them the book of cloth samples, they flipped through it for an hour and a half—and they still couldn't decide what they wanted."

"'Morning, girls." Sebastiano sauntered up to his locker, whistling. "Some rockin' party at Mo's on Saturday, huh?" He spun his lock open, then looked up at the girls. Holly could feel Lina making "shut up! shut up!" faces at him.

"What?" Sebastiano said. Then he looked at Holly. "Whoa, Frankenstein, what happened to you?"

"What are you talking about?" Holly asked.

"Those circles under your eyes. Rough night?"

"I worked all day on my history project," Holly said. "I stayed up pretty late, I guess. I got such a late start—"

"It's due next week, you know," Sebastiano said. "It's

only worth fifty percent of our grade."

"I know, Sebastiano," Holly said. "So Mo's was good?"

"Yeah—where were you?" Sebastiano said. "All that bash needed was a little pinch of Holly. The food! They had a burrito bar, shrimp, burgers—veggie and regular—homemade blueberry pie. . . . It was better than a bar mitzvah—!"

"Sebastiano—" Lina began, but Holly shushed her.

"Let the boy speak," she said. She knew he would hold nothing back. He was reliable that way.

"They had really good beer—not the usual swill—and everybody was swimming, and then Autumn jumped in the pool and her top fell off and she didn't care. She didn't even bother to put it back on!—that's how blissed out everybody was—and—"

"Okay, you can stop now." Holly gave Lina a mock-mean glare. "So, I guess I can't count on you for the scoop."

"I just didn't want you to feel bad," Lina said.

"I know," Holly said. "It's really my own fault that I missed the best party of the year and stayed up all night reading about the Grand Duchess Anastasia. I can't let Julia push me around. This has got to stop."

16 Elvira Confesses

To:	linaonme
From:	your daily horoscope

HERE IS TODAY'S HOROSCOPE: CANCER: You may think you've found the truth, but don't be so sure. Your search for truth ends when I say so, and not before. Got it?

"Why are you doing this to me?" Lina finallly found Ramona at her locker at the end of the day.

"Doing what?" Ramona asked, smoothing the Donald Death poster inside her locker before slamming the door shut.

"Stop denying it," Lina said. "I know it was you."

"Are you talking about that Elvira thing? I told you

already it wasn't me. I told Mads, too. You don't need to sic your dopey friends on me trying to spook the truth out of me."

Lina sighed. Why was Ramona being so stubborn? Usually she was proud of her sneaky, conniving mind.

"Listen, Ramona," Lina said. "Please, just admit what you did. Walker is still angry about it. No matter what I say, he thinks *I'm* Elvira. And he won't listen to me. But if I can tell him who was really behind the whole thing, and convince him that I had nothing to do with it, maybe he'll forgive me. And then we can be friends again. Don't you see how important this is?"

"I do see," Ramona said. "But I didn't do it."

Lina slumped against the tiny metal lockers. "I wish I could believe you," she said. "But I just can't think of anyone else who had the ability and the motive to commit the crime. There's no one but you."

"That can't be true," Ramona said. "There must be someone else, because I'm not Elvira!"

"Come on, Ramona, stop it," Lina said. She could tell Ramona was lying. She exhibited all the signs: nervousness, lack of eye contact, constant brushing of hair out of eyes. Of course, she did that all the time, but still. Why didn't she just confess?

"I'm going to tell Walker on you, anyway," Lina said.

"So you might as well come clean."

Ramona pressed her back against the lockers and picked at a rip in her Spanish workbook.

"You really like him, don't you," she said.

"Yes, I do," Lina said. "Even though he doesn't like me right now. I'm trying to change that."

"All right," Ramona said. "I admit it. I wrote that mean X-Rating. I'm Elvira."

Lina grimaced. "Why did you wait so long to confess?" she asked.

"I guess I just thought I'd hide behind the character I created," Ramona said.

"I know you were trying to help," Lina said. "But you totally screwed everything up. You've got to find Walker right now and explain everything."

"Can't I do it tomorrow?" Ramona asked.

"He's at the pool covering a swim meet," Lina said. "Go on, just get it over with. The sooner you tell him you're Elvira, the sooner he'll forgive me."

"I swear I'll do it later," Ramona said. "I don't feel like going to the Swim Center. Chlorine gives me a terrible headache—"

"Quit stalling." Lina grabbed Ramona by the back of her army jacket and started pulling her down the hall. Ramona was trying to squirm out of an unpleasant duty, and Lina was determined to make sure she confessed. "I'll take you to him myself, just to be sure you don't pull some other trick—like trying to blame all this on Autumn or somebody." Ramona was not one of Autumn's biggest fans.

"It *would* be funny if we told him Autumn did it," Ramona said. "And then Walker would be mad at her, and she would be mad at you, and the chain reaction could lead to a huge explosion!"

"No." Lina marched Ramona out of the main building, down the path leading to the gym, and into the Swim Center. Walker was sitting in the bleachers watching the team warm up for a meet.

"Walker, Ramona has something to say to you." Lina shoved Ramona in front of Walker. He looked up at Ramona, then Lina, surprised and annoyed.

"What now?" he said.

Lina gave Ramona a little pinch. That was her cue to start talking.

"Walker, I have to tell you something," Ramona said.

"I know," Walker said. "Lina just said that."

"Um, okay." Ramona glanced longingly at the swimmers in the pool as if she wished she could jump in, clothes and all, and swim away. "You know that X-Rating that said all those terrible things about you and Flynn?"

Walker's eyes darkened, and his back straightened. "Yes?"

"Well, the first and most important thing you should know is, Lina didn't write it. She had nothing to do with it. Really."

"And—" Lina coached, egging her on.

"And, anyway—not that you'd care or anything—but I wrote it. I made it all up. Including the name Elvira. Who is me." She stopped to check Walker's reaction. The look on his face was stony. She instinctively shrank back from him. "So I'm sorry. Okay? I'm really sorry. Please forgive Lina. It's all my fault!"

"Really? It's all your fault?" Walker said icily. "Why would you do something like that? What would you have to gain from it?"

"Well, nothing personally, but Lina is my friend, and I care about her, and I did a tarot card reading one night and the cards said that you and Lina are made for each other, so you might as well stop fighting it and forgive Lina for whatever it is you're mad at her about."

"A tarot card reading?" Walker snorted. "Stop jerking me around, Ramona. You, too, Lina. You probably put Ramona up to this. You either made her confess to writing it when you really did, or you made her write it for you. Either way, the real mastermind here is you. Isn't it?"

"What are you talking about?" Lina cried. "Mastermind? You know, you're making a bigger deal out of this than—"

A whistle blew, and the meet began. "Excuse me, girls, but I have a meet to cover," Walker said.

Lina ran out of the Swim Center, Ramona at her heels. "Can you believe him?" Lina cried. "Even after you confessed to everything, he's still mad at *me*! I didn't do *anything*!"

"You know, that was true what I said about the tarot cards," Ramona said. "They really did say you guys were meant for each other."

"What?" Lina snapped. "Shut up. That's the last thing I want to hear right now. I'm so pissed!"

"Maybe he doesn't want to be friends with you," Ramona said.

"That's fine with me," Lina said. "If he doesn't want to be friends, then neither do I. There, it's official. Walker and I are no longer friends!"

17 The Mystery of 1972

To:	mad4u
From:	your daily horoscope

HERE IS TODAY'S HOROSCOPE: VIRGO: The answers are out there, but you won't find them on the Home Shopping Network.

Mads hopped on her bike and headed to the town library. She'd spent the morning searching the online archives of the *Crier* for old articles about Rosewood. She hoped there might be something in the history of the school that would help her case when she presented it to the parents' board.

And she thought she'd found something. She had to go all the way back to 1972, but there were a few obscure references to some kind of fight or scandal at RSAGE involving the students and self-expression. The paper didn't say exactly what had happened, but it did mention that the entire senior class got detention. So it must have been big.

The Carlton Bay Public Library had a collection of yearbooks for every school in the area, dating back to the late nineteenth century. Mads hoped the 1972 yearbook might give her a clue about the scandal. She skimmed the long row of rose-colored yearbook spines, *The Garden Gate*, year after year after year. What had happened in 1972 that would cause the whole class to get detention? She ran her finger through the seventies—'70, '71, '73 . . . Where was 1972?

Someone must have checked it out, Mads thought. She went to the librarian's desk to find out.

"No, the yearbooks are reference," the librarian said. "No one is allowed to check them out. Which issue is missing?"

"The Rosewood *Garden Gate*, 1972," Mads said.

"Oh. You know, it's funny, but we don't have that year," the librarian said. "The school never gave the library a copy of it."

"Do you know why?" Mads asked. The librarian was in her thirties, Mads guessed—too young to have been in high school in 1972.

She shook her head. "No, I have no idea. We simply don't have it. Maybe the students didn't issue a yearbook that year? A lot of weird things happened in those days, especially with students. You know: protests, upheaval, lots of changes. . . ."

"I read something in an old issue of the *Crier* about a scandal at Rosewood that year," Mads said. "I was hoping to find out more about it."

The librarian shrugged. "Well, all I can tell you is, try the school library. Or Rosewood's records room, in the basement of the library. They might have a copy of the missing yearbook, or something on file that explains what happened."

"Thanks." Mads sat down at a carrel to think about this. No yearbook for one year, and one year only? Could that have been a punishment for whatever it was that the seniors did that year? It was very strange.

There's a story here, Mads thought. *There's something to this—I just know it. I've got to find that yearbook.*

18 Are You a Pushover?

To:	hollygolitely
From:	your daily horoscope

HERE IS TODAY'S HOROSCOPE: CAPRICORN: Someone is bringing out your inner wimp, and it's not a pretty sight.

"Julia, I have to talk to you about something," Holly said. She sat in the Safrans' kitchen while Julia flipped through her wedding planner notebook.

"I have *so* much to talk to you about, too," Julia said. "Do you think the bridesmaids should wear heels or flats? Deirdre is pretty tall—she'll tower over all the ushers in heels—but on the other hand—"

"Julia, wait," Holly said. "I love helping you with your wedding and everything—"

"Do you? I'm so glad. Because I love doing it with you. Imagine if I had to do this all by myself? I'd lose my mind! But also, it wouldn't be nearly as much fun."

Holly took a deep breath and tried again. "It is fun, but the thing is, I've got other stuff to do, and I don't have much time to help you now. We've gotten a lot done already, and Deirdre and Bethany are here. Don't you think you could handle the rest without me?"

Julia was finally quiet, and Holly suddenly wished she'd start babbling again. She stared at Holly with hurt in her round brown eyes.

"But I'm having so much fun with you," Julia said. "Aren't you?"

"Sure, I am," Holly said. "It's just that I'm so busy myself. Don't you remember what high school is like? It's getting toward the end of the semester. I've got big projects to work on, and one of my best friends just got suspended because of our blog. I'm getting testimonials from dozens of kids trying to clear her name, and on top of that, there are parties and family stuff—"

"It's just—I'm afraid," Julia said. "This is one of the biggest moments of my life. I want you to be part of it. You have such awesome taste. You always know what you like, and you're always right. If I have to choose between crab cakes or mini hot dogs, I get paralyzed. I—I need your opinion, that's all. Please, Holly—I *need* you."

Holly simply didn't want to do wedding stuff anymore. But she didn't know how to say it without hurting Julia.

"Hello, girls." Mrs. Safran shuffled into the kitchen in her robe and slippers. "I thought I'd make some tea."

She put a kettle on the stove and said, "Holly, I'm glad you're here. I just wanted to thank you for all you've done for Julia. You have no idea how much it means to her, to me—to all of us."

Holly took a quavery breath. Oh, god.

"I'm sure you're aware that we're all going through a—a transition period," Mrs. Safran said. Holly nodded and looked down at the table. Julia took her hand. Mrs. Safran took the other hand. "And having you around has been just wonderful. It's so good for Rob. And I've felt terrible that I haven't been able to help Julia plan her big day as much as I'd like. But knowing you're here with her makes it easier." She squeezed Holly's hand. "We all love you so much. It's like you're part of the family."

Holly swallowed. *I'm doomed,* she thought. *There's no way out.* She managed a weak smile. "I love you all, too. I feel so at home here," she said.

The kettle whistled. Mrs. Safran gave Holly's hand a firm pat. "Well, good. Things will pick up for us soon. In the meantime, we're grateful to you."

"And she has great taste, too, Mom," Julia said.

"She's an angel." Mrs. Safran poured herself a cup of tea and shuffled back toward her room. "Good night!"

"Rob, please." Holly gave it one more shot when Rob drove her home a few hours later. "I can't take any more wedding stuff! Julia won't make a single decision on her own—she leaves everything up to me!"

"I know, she is so bridal," Rob said. "Like, possessed or something. Believe me, I get it all the time, too. 'Rob, call the tuxedo rental place. Rob, make sure Michael remembers the ring. Rob, get a haircut. Blah blah blah blah blah.'" Rob and Gabe were going to be ushers.

"See? And I'm not in the family. I'm not even in the wedding," Holly said. "Can't you talk to Julia for me and get her to ease up a little? Whenever I try, she pulls a guilt trip on me about how I'm holding your family together single-handedly."

"But Holls, it's been fun having you around all the time," Rob said. "And if I've got to suffer through it, it's so much nicer to have you suffering with me."

"How sweet," Holly joked.

"It will all be over in a couple of weeks," Rob said. "Until then, think of what you're doing, you unselfish girl. You're making Julia happy, which makes Mom happy, which makes me happy. . . . You're helping us through our hard time." He pulled up in front of her house and stopped the car. "Without you, it would be torture." He brushed her hair out of her face and kissed her. "And now, finally, we are alone."

"Finally," Holly said. She wasn't a big fan of the car make-out session, but she'd take what she could get.

Rob put her seat back until it was almost flat, then climbed over to her side. He pressed against her, and they kissed until the windows steamed up. She pulled off her sweater, and he nuzzled her through her thin t-shirt.

"You're so hot," he murmured, sliding his hand under her shirt. Then his face literally lit up, caught in someone's high beams. A car had pulled up behind them. He quickly pulled his hand away. "Someone's home."

Holly sat up and squinted into the headlights. It was her father, coming home late from work.

"Okay, that was totally embarrassing," Rob said.

"I don't think he saw anything," Holly said.

"No, just me on top of his daughter in a car," Rob said.

"Even if he noticed, he won't say anything," Holly said. "Or he might, just to tease me. It's no big deal."

She straightened her clothes and smoothed her hair. "Guess I'd better go inside."

"See you at the next wedding meeting," he said. She frowned. "Kidding," he added. "Good night." He kissed her one more time. The heat was still there.

Oh, Rob, she thought. *How can I say no to you?*

She couldn't. That was the problem.

QUIZ: ARE YOU A PUSHOVER?

Sure, you want to do nice things for your friends, but where do you draw the line? Are you just being a good pal—or is she taking advantage of you?

1. Oh, no! Your friend broke her leg. You:

a ▶ visit her every day, bring her treats, and fill her in on the gossip she missed.

b ▶ tell her you'll see her when the cast comes off—if she ever walks again.

c ▶ volunteer to become her live-in nurse/butler.

2. Your friend hasn't finished her history paper—and it's due tomorrow! She calls you up crying—she'll get an F! You:

a ▶ encourage her to calm down and get as much done as she can. Maybe the teacher will give her an extension.

b ▶ tell her you'd love to talk, but *The O.C.* is on.

c ▶ stay up all night writing the paper for her.

3. A cute guy approaches you and your friend at a party. You really like him, and so does she. You:

a ▶ wait to see which one of you he's interested in.

b ▶ battle her to the death over him.

c ▶ bow out gracefully and let her have him—after all, the guy she's already dating isn't really working out.

4. There's a big party tonight, and your friend has nothing to wear. You:

a ▶ offer to go shopping with her or lend her something of yours.

b ▶ tell her the sweat-stained workout clothes she has on look fine.

c ▶ give her the new dress you were going to wear—it looks better on her, anyway.

5. Your friend's parents are driving her crazy—they won't let her do anything! You:

a ▶ commiserate—parents can be so clueless.

b ▶ tell her you weren't listening—what is she crying about again?

c ▶ have a serious talk with her parents and tell them if they don't shape up you'll find a way to make them.

6. **A boy she likes told her she's ugly. She's upset. You:**
   - **a ▶ reassure her that she's beautiful and that the boy must be blind.**
   - **b ▶ tell her he's right, she is ugly (it's time she faced the truth).**
   - **c ▶ hire someone to break the boy's fingers.**

Scoring:

Mostly a's: You're a good friend with a good heart and a well-balanced sense of responsibility. Keep on keeping on.

Mostly b's: You're a terrible friend and way too mean! Be nicer or soon you won't have any friends to kick around.

Mostly c's: You're a total pushover. You're practically your friend's slave! Get a life and let her deal with her own problems.

19 Kissing Is Good

To:	linaonme
From:	your daily horoscope

HERE IS TODAY'S HOROSCOPE: CANCER: There's no air freshener on the market that covers the stench of desperation, so you can stop looking.

"Oh. You're here."

Lina stepped into *The Seer* late in the afternoon to do some research for Mads. She was hoping the school paper's old files might hold a clue to the missing yearbook mystery. She'd thought it would be safe; she'd thought everyone would be gone by then. But one lone writer sat in the office, typing on his laptop. Walker. Of course.

Walker looked up. "Yes. I'm here."

"I've got some work to do." Lina went to a file cabinet across the room and opened a drawer marked 1970-75. She wasn't about to leave just because he was there. He couldn't push her around. "If you don't mind."

"Knock yourself out."

Lina riffled through the files, trying to concentrate, but the tension in the office was as thick as hair gel. She struggled not to let her eyes stray across the room to see what Walker was doing. But it was hopeless.

The clicking of his keyboard stopped. She couldn't help it. She glanced over. Was he looking at her? Not really. The clicking started again. Lina sighed. The old *Seer* files were sloppily kept and incomplete. She couldn't concentrate. Maybe she needed some caffeine. She crossed the room to a mini fridge where Kate sometimes kept sodas and juice.

"I'm just getting something to drink," she said as she brushed past Walker's desk.

"It's a free country," Walker said.

"That's right," Lina said. She opened the fridge. Empty.

"You seem to feel pretty free," Walker said. "Free to spread lies about people on your blog. Free to butt into other people's business—"

She walked up to him and pressed her hands on his desk. "I never butted into your business."

Walker stood up to face her. "Oh, no?"

"No," Lina said. "And I never lied on my blog. I told you, I had nothing to do with that Elvira thing."

"Then what was it doing on your blog?"

She leaned toward him to make sure he got her point. "Ramona put it there without my permission. How many times do I have to tell you that?"

"You can tell it to me a zillion times and I'll never believe it."

"Believe whatever you want. I don't care."

Now he leaned closer to her. "I will. I believe you don't care about a lot of things. Like hurting people's feelings. And messing up people's lives."

"I explained that! Why won't you listen to me? You're so rigid! You're unfair!" She stuck her face close to his.

"You're unfair! And you break your word!" His face came closer.

"What? I do not!"

"You do, too. And you know what else? Your writing is packed with clichés. You overuse the underdog cliché in every story. It's the hokiest device in sportswriting!" His angry face slowly moved closer and closer to hers. They were like a baseball player and an umpire arguing over a bad call. *I do not use clichés! I hate him!* Lina thought. *I hate him! He's horrible!*

"Well, *you* like mean, bitchy girls who brag!" she shot

back. "And you're a bad speller!"

"Better than you!"

"I challenge you to a spell-off!"

"You're on!"

They were nearly nose-to-nose now. Lina could smell his breath—minty. She opened her mouth to say, "I'll spell rings around you," but the words never came out.

She opened her lips, and the next thing she knew, his were there, too. And they were kissing.

Lina closed her eyes. Her anger melted away in a wave of delicious kissing. His lips were so soft. His tongue lightly flicked against her teeth.

She opened her eyes. He opened his. They stared at each other, surprised.

That was one hell of a kiss.

She straightened up. *Wow. Let's do that again.* She reached for him. What was she so mad about, anyway?

But his eyes were wide with shock. He smiled, then blinked.

"I—I've got to go," he mumbled. He grabbed his things and ran out of the room.

Lina stared at the door. She glanced around the empty room. What had just happened? What was that all about?

Kissing was good! It was a good thing.

So why did he run away?

20 Breaking and Entering

To:	mad4u
From:	your daily horoscope

HERE IS TODAY'S HOROSCOPE: VIRGO: Did you think the universe had forgotten about you? Nah, it was just waiting for the right time to toss a bolt of lightning your way.

El Diario in Exile
by Madison "Solzhenitsyn" Markowitz

I am mounting a big defense of the Dating Game and I need your help. First: Please remember to come to the big rally this Thursday at 7! And second: Please write in with any comments or stories about the Dating Game, how it helped you, what you like about it, what you've gotten from it, anything! Did you find your true love through us? Did you have a few good dates? Did you at least get some funny stories out of it to tell at parties? We will use your stories to show the parents and administration that RSAGE needs the Dating Game and that it plays an important part in student life.

We'll post your responses in the space below as they come in:

nuclearautumn: I always thought mads, lina, and holly were kind of, I dunno, nobodies? I mean, they weren't really unpopular but they weren't überpopular, either, and basically I didn't notice them. when I filled out a matchmaking questionnaire on the dating game I expected to get matched with loser after loser, which I would then throw back in the girls' faces to make them see how inferior they were. But I was so wrong! On the first try (it took them a while, but still) they matched me with my sweet little vince, and we've been together ever since. (hey, that rhymes!) We can't keep our hands off each other! So I have to admit the dating game changed my life in a big way for the better, and I hate to see poor mads getting punished for it—I mean, alvarado and the parents' board are going a little overboard, don't you think? —Autumn Nelson

gogo90: Whenever I feel down, I go to the dating game.

Sometimes I think nobody likes me and I'm the world's biggest loser, but when I read the dating game I see even the most popular people in school are looking for someone or something. it's a leveler. Everybody's insecure about something, and the dating game lays it all out there. bring it back, you heartless scum!

throb: I wrote to the love ninja for advice about stuff I was scared to talk to anybody about. like when I thought my girlfriend was cheating on me with my best friend, and the ninja told me not to jump to conclusions and how to tell for sure. It turned out I was wrong, but I could have lost my girlfriend and my best friend if I'd done what I was thinking of doing, which was rolling them up in the wrestling mat and dumping them in the bay (not really, but I was pissed).

bleeblah: The dating game is real, it's fun, I'm totally addicted to it, it's like a glue that pulls the school together. Everybody is into it, from the loneliest dillweed to the brainest nerd to the most popular jock. It makes going to RSAGE mean something.

paco: The dating game broke my heart. But I still wouldn't trade my few happy moments with the love of my life,

> **the mind-bogglingly sexy madison markowitz, for anything. And it did inspire me to write lots and lots of poetry.**

Mads hovered at the edge of the campus, watching. It was four-fifteen on Tuesday afternoon, and the main school building was quiet. Most of the activity, Mads knew, was taking place deeper into the campus, in the auditorium, the Swim Center, and the athletic fields. Rod may or may not have gone home for the day. Ann Wilson, the librarian, usually left at four.

The yearbook mystery was driving her crazy. Lina had found some letters and articles in *The Seer* archives that mentioned the yearbook scandal, but they didn't explain exactly what had happened. The parents' board meeting was Thursday night. Time was running out. On a whim, Mads rode her bike to school. She was going to sneak into the library and find the missing yearbook.

Mads hurried down the front walk and ducked inside the building. She looked around to make sure no one had seen her before closing the door.

She walked through the quiet halls. The library lights were out, and Mrs. Wilson, the librarian, was gone. Mads slipped inside. She could see just well enough with the afternoon sunlight from the windows. She ducked behind the librarian's desk and looked around. There were a few books shelved under and around the checkout counter, but none of them were yearbooks.

Behind the checkout counter were the librarian's office and the door that led downstairs to the records room. Mads tried the door. It wasn't locked. Thank goodness—she didn't need breaking and entering added to her list of crimes.

The records room was pitch-dark. Mads flicked on the lights. The room had no windows, so no one would see the light from outside. There were rows of metal file cabinets and shelves of books, old and new—histories of Carlton Bay, of Northern California, and of the Rosewood School. And then, yes, there were the yearbooks. Mads read each year carefully. But once again, 1972 was missing.

Rats, she thought. *What the hell—?*

Maybe Mrs. Wilson kept it hidden somewhere. Maybe she had a secret place where she stashed controversial, scandal-related items. Mads didn't know the librarian well, but she had a sense of her as a woman who believed in truth and respected history. Someone who would want to preserve anything that told the real story. But Mads could be wrong.

She turned out the lights and went back upstairs to Mrs. Wilson's office. She checked the drawers of her desk.

One of them was locked. The rest held nothing more interesting than a few paper clips and rubber bands.

Then she saw the cupboard. Hanging over a wall of file cabinets was a small wooden cupboard. It could only be reached with a ladder, or maybe a chair.

Mads pulled a chair over and climbed up. She could barely reach the cupboard. So she climbed up on the file cabinet beneath it and perched there precariously. She opened the cabinet door. Inside were books and papers stashed haphazardly. Mads rummaged through them until she felt a thick, heavy book with a textured cover. She pulled it out. Bingo! The 1972 *Garden Gate*!

Mads shut the cupboard door, scrambled off the file cabinet, and sat down to flip through the book. What was the big scandal? Why would they hide an innocent yearbook?

Everything looked normal: photos of the teachers, the campus, the underclassmen. A portrait of each senior, and group shots of the sports teams, clubs, and other organizations. Here and there antiwar slogans had been slipped into the captions, and some students flashed peace signs or wore t-shirts with slogans protesting the war or the draft or conformity. Other than that, it was funny to see how the students of those days didn't look so different from Mads and her friends. A lot of the fashions and hairstyles were similar, though the 1972 boys looked thinner and less buff than the current boys.

There was a picture of Mrs. Wilson in her office, smiling and looking strangely young. Then, near the end, Mads turned the page and found the senior class photo. Her hand flew to her mouth to keep from making too much noise.

"Oh, my god—"

The class had posed under a banner that said CLASS OF 72 SAYS DRAFT THIS! But that wasn't the shocking part. The shocker was that the whole, entire class was mooning the camera!

Mads started laughing. This was the big scandal? No wonder the library didn't want to make this public. But still, it wasn't that big a deal. Just a joke. The school ought to have more of a sense of humor. Then Mads thought about her own situation and realized it wasn't so different.

Then she remembered that Rod was in this class. Was he in the picture, too?

No faces were visible, obviously. Just bottoms. Mads flipped to the front of the yearbook and found the masthead, where the editorial credits were listed. Aha!

Editor in Chief: John Alvarado!

Rod was the editor of the yearbook. He was actually responsible for the scandalous photo! She laughed again.

They never had naked butts on the Dating Game—not even close! What a hypocrite!

Mads got to her feet and stuffed the yearbook under her coat. Mission accomplished. Time to get out of there.

21 Pea-Green Wedding Cake

To:	hollygolitely
From:	your daily horoscope

HERE IS TODAY'S HOROSCOPE: CAPRICORN: Is it my imagination, or has your good judgment flown right out the window?

Tuesday afternoon, Julia dragged Holly back to the cake designer to confirm the cake details. But now Holly had a plan. All Julia lacked was a little confidence. She needed to see that her own taste was as good as Holly's. Holly planned to make the point as clearly as possible.

"Okay," Carmen said. "You've finally settled on chocolate cake with vanilla icing. Right? Please say yes."

Julia glanced at Holly, who nodded and tried to wave the responsibility for answering away from herself and back toward Julia. "Yes," Julia said.

"Good. Now for the decorations. We can tint the icing any color you like." She looked at Holly expectantly, as she was used to the answers coming from her.

"Julia's the bride," Holly said. "Julia?"

Julia looked at Holly and panicked. "Any color? Any color I want?"

"Well, there are certain colors we don't recommend," Carmen said. "But it's your call."

Clearly Julia was not going to pick up the ball. "We'll just sit down over there and think about it a minute," Holly told Carmen.

"Fine," Carmen said. "But I'm not letting you leave without a decision."

"Don't worry, we won't," Holly said. She led Julia to a little sitting area. "Do you have a color preference?" Holly asked her. "Think back to when you were a little girl, dreaming about your wedding. What color was the cake?"

Julia closed her eyes and thought back. "Um, I can't really see the cake. The groom, George Clooney, is blocking the way."

Holly sighed. Here we go, time to start Plan A. "I have a great idea. What do you think of this: pea green."

"Pea green what?"

"Pea green wedding cake," Holly said. "Do you love it? Remember that article we saw in *Bride*'s magazine about unusual colors for cakes? All the celebrities are doing it. I think Jennifer Lopez had a puce cake at her last wedding."

"Really?" Julia said. "Pea green?"

She'll never go for this, Holly thought. *She's got to realize that pea green cake is a terrible idea. And then she'll see that she doesn't need me so much after all.*

"You think pea green might be good?" Julia seemed doubtful. *Good,* Holly thought. *Trust your gut, Julia. Trust your instincts for once, for god's sake.*

Holly nodded. "Mmm-hmm. It's, like, so ugly, it's beautiful."

"Yeah," Julia said. "I can see that."

"Have you decided?" Carmen asked.

"Yes, I have," Julia said. "The icing should be pea green. With what color flowers, Holly?"

"Mustard yellow?" Holly sank into her seat in despair. She couldn't believe Julia would actually go for a pea green wedding cake. *I can't let her do this*, she thought. *I'll have to call Carmen later and change the icing color again. She'll probably hang up on me.* This was going to be harder than she'd thought.

On to the dress shop. Julia still hadn't decided on the bridesmaids' material.

"It's an evening wedding, isn't it?" Melissa asked. Holly had a feeling Melissa was getting as impatient with Julia as she was. "What about a dark color?"

Julia flipped through the fabric samples. Holly didn't need to look at them—she had the whole sample book memorized. "Yeah," Julia said, stopping on the last swatch: solid, plain black silk. "What about black? It's kind of elegant."

"Black could be good," Holly said. "Julia, I'm sure whatever you decide will be great. Just pick something. Anything."

"I think . . . black. But, wait—midnight blue!"

Holly couldn't take any more. She was afraid the top of her head was going to blow off from all the steam building up inside her. "You know what I think would be so cool?" she said, snatching up the sample book. She let the book fall open at random. Whatever fabric showed up, that's what Julia would have. And then it would be settled and they could get out of there. Holly hoped she never had to set foot in that dress shop again.

The book opened on polka dots—white silk with big red and blue polka dots. It was hideous. Holly didn't care. She barely even looked at it. She presented it triumphantly to Julia as if it were the answer to their prayers. "*This* is what your bridesmaids should wear," Holly said. "Gigantic polka dots!"

Julia blinked. Melissa sighed, said, "I've got a few calls to make," and left the room. Holly understood. The fabric was ridiculous. It looked as if it were made for a clown suit. If this didn't spur Julia to start making her own decisions, nothing would.

"Polka dots?" Julia took the book and stared at the swatch. "I don't know—"

Good, good, Holly thought. *Think for yourself, that's right. . . .*

"But black would be so easy to wear."

"That's true," Holly said. "But it's so ordinary. It's boring. Polka dots—now that's different."

She crossed her fingers. *Listen to how stupid I sound,* she silently said to Julia. *Can't you see how bad my ideas are? I'm no help to you—no help at all. In fact, you'd be better off making these wedding decisions yourself and leaving me to live my life of studying and parties without the thrill of constant wedding planning. Okay?*

"You know," Julia said, and Holly pleaded, pleaded for her to see the light. "Polka dots—it's very unusual. Almost weird."

Yes, yes . . .

"That's what I love about it!" Julia finished. Holly's heart sank. "You're right, Holly. As always. Giant polka dots. It's a great idea!"

Holly wanted to smack herself in the forehead. Pea

green cake? Clown suits for the bridesmaids? Her ideas were terrible! How could Julia keep agreeing with her? What would it take to get her to think for herself just once?

"Julia, wait," Holly said. "Think for a minute. You don't really want polka-dotted bridesmaids, do you?"

Julia thought it over. "Yes. Yes, I think I do."

"No, you don't."

"But you just said—"

"I know, but on second thought, maybe Melissa is right," Holly said. "Black. It's easy."

"No, I think I like the polka dots," Julia said.

Oh, okay. *Now* she's decisive. *Now* she wants to think for herself.

"I think the black works better," Holly said.

"But you said polka dots before," Julia said. "God, Holly, make up your mind."

22 Most Likely to Meddle

To: linaonme
From: your daily horoscope

HERE IS TODAY'S HOROSCOPE: CANCER: Today you will find out that—whoops!—you were wrong all along. From now on, why not begin with that assumption and save us all the time and trouble?

"See? I told you," Ramona said. "You and Walker were meant to be. The tarot never lies." She and Lina were sitting in the courtyard during a free period Wednesday, leaning against a big tree.

"Oh, yeah?" Lina said. "Well, what's going to happen next? What does it mean when you kiss a guy—after a blistering argument where you hurl insults at each other—

and then he runs away? Huh? Do the cards have an answer for that?"

"I'm sure they do," Ramona said. "If you want, I'll ask them when I get home."

"Don't bother," Lina said. "But you know what I *would* like? Next time, before you try to 'help' me by trashing somebody's reputation, *Elvira*, would you mind asking me first? To make sure I *want* that person's reputation trashed? Or better yet, just assume that I don't, and don't do it."

Ramona looked annoyed. "You shouldn't be so snotty with me," she said. "I've never done anything but help you."

"Right. Help me," Lina said. "Posing as Walker's ex-girlfriend and writing a fake X-Rating about him was a big help. Since then we've been *inseparable*."

"He kissed you, didn't he?"

"Yeah, and then he ran away, and I haven't seen him since. It's not exactly *Love Story*."

Someone chuckled from the other side of the tree trunk. Lina panicked—anyone could be sitting there right now listening to every word they said! Please, not Walker! Or Flynn!

"Hi, girls." Sebastiano poked his head around the tree.

"Oh, it's only you," Lina said.

"Only me! That hurts," Sebastiano said.

"I didn't mean it like that," Lina said.

"I know. Look, I think this charade has gone on long enough," Sebastiano said. "I can't let Ramona take credit for my work anymore."

"What are you talking about?" Lina asked.

"Ramona wasn't Elvira," Sebastiano said. "I was."

"*You* were!" Lina was shocked. "But Ramona confessed."

"I know," Sebastiano said. "Ramona, how dare you! I'm sure it was tempting—my plan was so clever, and it worked. But, still—it's not right."

Lina was confused. "Ramona—you weren't Elvira?"

"I tried to tell you that, but you wouldn't believe me," Ramona said.

"She *thinks* she's all diabolical, but really I'm the sneaky one," Sebastiano said. "Maybe the next time someone anonymously helps you, you'll think of me first."

"He works in the office once in a while, too, you know," Ramona said. "He has access to the same codes I do. You might have at least considered him as a suspect before jumping all over me."

"But why did you confess?" Lina asked.

"Because you didn't believe me, anyway, so what difference did it make? And I was sick of having the same conversation over and over." She made her voice higher to imitate Lina or Mads—it was hard to tell which. "'Ramona, stop lying! You're Elvira!' I had better things to do."

Lina felt terrible. She'd been so hard on Ramona. "I didn't realize you had it in you, Sebastiano."

"Neither did I," Ramona said.

"And I didn't think you cared that much," Lina said. "About my love life, I mean."

"Well, I couldn't watch you and Walker fight the way you did at the softball game and do *nothing*," Sebastiano said. "What kind of heartless cad do you think I am?"

"Well—" Lina said.

"You do think I'm a heartless cad, don't you!" Sebastiano cried. "I'm—I'm *stung*."

"No, of course, I don't think you're heartless," Lina said. "Right, Ramona?"

"Not heartless, just a gi-normous busy body," Ramona said. "Congratulations, Sebastiano. You move to the top of our Most Likely to Meddle list. Are you thrilled?"

"Oh, I am," Sebastiano said. "It's an honor."

23 Big Polka-dotted Surprise

To:	hollygolitely
From:	your daily horoscope

HERE IS TODAY'S HOROSCOPE: CAPRICORN: If you had to do it all over again, you wouldn't change a thing. Right? How dumb can you get?

"Holly, come to my room," Julia said. "I have a big surprise for you and I don't want to announce it here in the sunroom with those oafs watching some horrible reality TV show. It's too big for that."

Too big? What could it be? Holly had arrived at the Safrans' house after school on Wednesday determined to be with Rob and Rob alone, no matter what Julia tried to rope her into. She and Rob were warm under the afghan and she hated to get up. The afghan covered up all kinds of fun activities. Besides, once Julia got her into her room, who knew what diabolical wedding chores she might dream up for her?

"You can tell me here, can't you?" Holly said. "Whatever it is, I'm just going to tell Rob, anyway."

"You can tell Rob after I tell you," Julia said. "I think he'll be happy." She grabbed Holly by the hand and tried to yank her to her feet. "It's not a secret. It's just a big, important, exciting announcement."

Now that Holly was standing, the afghan puddled at her feet, she saw the futility of resistance. "Toss that blanket back up here, babe," Rob said. Holly covered him with the afghan. "And come back quick."

"I'll try," Holly said as Julia dragged her out of the sun room. Holly had to admit she was curious. This was a high level of excitement, even for Julia.

"You're going to be so thrilled," Julia said as she sat Holly on her bed. "Okay—are you ready?"

Holly nodded. "Ready."

"I want *you*"—she paused for effect—"to be my—"

"Personal assistant?" Holly guessed.

"Nooo—"

"Slave girl?"

"No." Julia laughed.

Go ahead and laugh, but it wasn't a joke, Holly thought.

"It's much better than that. I want you to be—my maid of honor!"

"Your what?" Holly was stunned. Maid of honor? She'd only known Julia for a few weeks. Wasn't that reserved for sisters and best friends?

"You've been such a good friend to me since I came home," Julia said, getting teary. "And such a big help. A huge help. I wouldn't even be getting married if it weren't for all you've done. Deirdre and Bethany have been completely useless."

"Well, gee, it wasn't—"

"Don't say it was nothing," Julia said. "You have such great taste, and you're so decisive and organized and smart. . . . I feel so lucky that you're my brother's girlfriend. You feel like a sister to me. The sister I never had."

Holly didn't know what to say. She felt guilty for her secret bad attitude toward Julia and all her tasks lately. Julia had a good heart, and she sincerely loved Holly. But still—maid of honor?

"Julia, I'm so flattered," Holly said. "But don't you have another friend, someone closer to you, whom you've known a little longer, that you'd rather have for your maid of honor? You know, a best friend or someone like that?"

"Oh—well, I used to," Julia said. "I did have a best friend . . . but I lost her."

"I'm sorry," Holly said, thinking, *Uh-oh—sore subject? Did her best friend die or something?* "What happened?"

"She's not speaking to me anymore," Julia explained. "I kind of—stole Michael from her."

"Your fiancé? You stole him from your best friend?"

"Yeah. It's pretty terrible, I guess. But he didn't love her, he loved me! What was I supposed to do? Walk away from the love of my life just because my best friend couldn't handle it?"

"That is a tough one," Holly said.

"So you're it. You're my best friend now," Julia said. "I love Deirdre and Bethany; of course I do. But they aren't as special to me as you are."

Holly had to admit that a part of her felt pretty good about this. It was an amazing honor, if you thought about it. So what if it meant more bridal chores? It was all in the name of a joyous occasion. As long as Julia didn't try to stab Holly in the back the way she did her best friend. But since Holly's boyfriend was Julia's brother, she was probably safe.

On the other hand . . .

"What about a dress?" Holly asked, thinking she'd found an out. "It's too late for a fitting now. I'll never get a dress made in time for the wedding."

Julia broke into a wide grin. "That's the best surprise of all," she said. "I took care of that—all by myself! With a little help from you, though you weren't aware of it." She went to the closet. "I already had a dress made. And I'm one hundred percent sure you're going to love it!"

Holly's stomach fluttered. She didn't like the sound of this.

"I finally made my decision about the dresses, you'll be relieved to know," Julia said. "I decided the bridesmaids should wear black after all. It *is* so elegant for an evening wedding."

Whew, Holly thought. *Dodged that one.*

"Good going!" Holly said, genuinely proud of her. "See, I told you you could decide these things on your own."

"Thank you," Julia said. "But I made another decision totally by myself. Since you're the maid of honor, you need to stand out from the other bridesmaids. So I had your dress made a little bit differently."

She reached into the closet and pulled out a gown—the most hideous dress Holly had ever seen. White silk with big blue and red polka dots. "Ta-da! It's the fabric you loved so much! Could you die?"

Holly's heart sank to her belly. *Yes, actually, I could.*

"I just knew you'd be excited. You loved the polka

dots best, I could tell. I know you told me to go with the black in the end, but your first instinct was polka dots. Wait until Rob sees you in this dress! Wait till *everybody* sees you! Just like you said, it's so unusual!"

"Yes, it is," Holly said. "It's unusual."

Julia made her look at the dress in the mirror. "What do you think?"

Holly held the dress up. *A little makeup, maybe a rainbow wig, and a red rubber nose, and it will be perfect,* she thought.

24 Moonshot

To:	mad4u
From:	your daily horoscope

HERE IS TODAY'S HOROSCOPE: VIRGO: Today will be one of your rare days of triumph. Enjoy it; then prepare to return to your usual state of mediocrity.

"Free speech for all!"

"Hell no, we won't shut up!"

"Hear us, don't smear us!"

"You ready, Mads?" Holly asked.

"Ready." Mads sat with Lina and Holly in the backseat of her parents' car, facing the huge crowd that had gathered outside Rosewood Thursday night. Lina and Holly had designated Mads chief speaker. Her big moment had come. Lina and Holly had done a lot to help the cause, interviewing students, gathering testimonials, and researching free-speech issues. But Mads was the one who was suspended. She had a lot to gain or lose from whatever happened that night.

Mads' mother kissed her. "Good luck, honey. We'll see you in there."

"Go get 'em, killer," Russell said.

Mads, Holly, and Lina hustled through the crowd to get inside the school. They were amazed at how many students—and kids from other schools, too—had shown up to protest and support them.

Mads' suspension had given her a lot of free time, and she'd used it. She read about the history of the First Amendment and thought hard about what she was going to say at this meeting. She wrote and rewrote her speech. She practiced it in front of Holly and Lina until it was as good as she could make it. And she was so nervous, she couldn't sleep the night before. She wanted the Dating Game reinstated, she wanted to make an important point about censorship, and she wanted her record cleared. But mostly, she wanted Rod and the parents' board to see that the students had the right to express themselves. It was a lot to ask for in one night.

The auditorium was packed with parents, teachers,

and students. Mads, Holly, and Lina joined Rod and Belinda Crocker, head of the parents' board, on the stage. Lina squeezed Mads' hand. "You nervous?"

"My stomach feels like it's full of cement."

Mads was given a special dispensation and allowed back on campus for this meeting. There were a few routine matters the board had to vote on first, and then it was on to the main event: what to do about the school's sex blog.

Belinda Crocker took the microphone. "There's too much talk about sex in our society," she said. "It's everywhere. The last thing our children need is more exposure to sex at school. That's why I fought to close this dating site down. Enough is enough! It's time the parents took charge of their children's lives. Kids, I'm sorry, but you don't know what's good for you. When I was in school, nothing like this ever happened. The adults shielded us from it. And that's the way I want it to be for my children."

She left the podium and sat down to a chorus of boos from the students and applause from some adults. Rod stood and took the mike.

"I'd like to clarify a few points," Rod said. "We are not trying to stifle student creativity or expression. We recently held a school art fair where all kinds of experimental work was displayed. But it is our opinion that this blog has gotten out of hand. Some students may be mature enough to handle the content of it, but some may not. I—"

"It's the parents who can't handle it!" a student yelled from the audience. This was met with wild cheers. Rod frowned.

"I will cancel this meeting if we cannot conduct it in a civilized manner," he warned. "To continue, the students may do as they please, or as their parents allow, off school property. But the school Web site is no place for frank discussions of the students' sexual lives. The members of the parents' board voted on this, and a majority agreed that they do not support this blog. Madison Markowitz, Lina Ozu, and Holly Anderson, the founders of the Dating Game, are here tonight to defend it and try to convince the board to reinstate it. I have warned them that it is futile, but to show the school's willingness to listen to its students, we have agreed to let them state their case. Girls?"

Mads stood and went to the podium, followed by Lina and Holly. Mads' knees wobbled. The cement in her stomach turned to ice.

The microphone squealed as Mads approached it. "Thank you, Mr. Alvarado," she said in a shaky voice. A giant screen hung behind her, and she held the clicker for a slide projector in her hand. If there was one thing she'd learned at RSAGE, it was that multimedia was the best way to get a point across. The first slide showed the Constitution and the Bill of Rights.

"From the beginning of American history, people have tried to challenge free speech," Mads said. "There will always be people who don't like what their fellow citizens say and do. Some people like to dye their hair that super-saturated, Raggedy Ann shade of red. Other people think it looks stupid. They have the right to express that disagreement. No one can tell you not to dye your hair Raggedy Ann red. No one can stop you from saying it looks dumb. And no one has the right to shut down a forum for free expression, whether it is a newspaper, an art show, or a Web site."

The students in the audience clapped.

"In the Constitution, students are guaranteed the same rights as their parents and teachers," Mads said. "But parents and school officials often try to squelch our voices. Maybe if they listened to us instead of tried to keep us quiet, we would understand each other better."

More applause. Mads was gaining confidence.

"The Dating Game was a place where students exchanged ideas. Some adults didn't approve of what we were saying, so they shut us down. Was that right?"

"No!" the audience shouted.

"I have come here tonight to ask you, the parents' board, and you, Mr. Alvarado, for two things. Bring back the Dating Game. And stop censoring us!"

The crowd cheered.

"We need a place to air our anxieties and insecurities and grievances. Sure, weird issues come up. Some kids are just weird. So are some adults. That's life. All that weird stuff exists whether we write about it or not. If you don't let us express our feelings freely, they will find other ways to come out—less healthy ways."

The students in the crowd cheered again. Mads glanced at Rod, who shifted in his seat. Belinda sat with her lips pursed tightly. Was she getting through to them? "You're doing great," Holly whispered.

"The Dating Game has helped make lots of students happier," Mads said. "And to prove it, first, we present our Parade of Happy Couples and Other Supporters."

Holly and Lina had gathered as many happily matched couples as they could find to march across the stage and testify on the Dating Game's behalf. Each couple, holding hands, stopped at the microphone, and made a brief speech.

"I'm Kris, and this is Jorge," a girl said. "Before I met Jorge, I had no friends. I spent all my free time writing fan letters to obscure actors and hoping they'd write back. Then I filled out a Dating Game questionnaire, and they matched me with Jorge. He taught me how to skateboard, and I taught him how to hunt down famous people's addresses. Jorge is my soul mate, but I never would have found him without the Dating Game."

"She's a wicked good skater," Jorge added.

Everyone clapped for them. Kris and Jorge beamed and walked off the stage.

"We're Autumn and Vince. Until the Dating Game matched us, no one would listen to me," Autumn said.

"And no one really talked to me," Vince said.

"Now we're really happy!" Autumn finished.

"I thought nobody would like me unless I was perfect," a pretty girl said. "But on the Dating Game, I found out that even the perfect girls don't think they're perfect. And that I have two secret admirers!"

After several more testimonials, Mads returned to the mike.

"This school is supposed to be a center of liberal education. It has a long and rich history of dissent. Some of the parents and teachers in this room were once like us, fighting for their right to express themselves."

She pressed the clicker, and a slide appeared on the screen. It showed a crowd of neatly dressed high school kids jammed into the Rosewood lunchroom. "In 1967, Rosewood students protested the dress code. Girls weren't allowed to wear pants to school. Can you believe that? And boys weren't allowed to have hair that reached below their collars. The students took over the cafeteria and refused to leave until the administration gave in. The students totally won. Of course! What a ridiculous dress code."

She pressed the clicker again and a page from an old copy of *The Seer* flashed on the screen. "Here's an article from our school newspaper dated May 14, 1972. 'Yearbooks Destroyed! Students Outraged at School Censorship.' The students had used their yearbook to protest the draft and the war in Vietnam. The school administration actually banned the yearbook! They wouldn't let the seniors have this important memento of their time at Rosewood. All because they didn't like the way the students had chosen to express their feelings. To this day, the 1972 yearbook is not available to the public. An outraged student wrote this in *The Seer*: 'As students, it is not only our right but our *duty* to upset the status quo. The status quo is unjust! We must do whatever we can make our world a better place. But we cannot do it unless we're allowed to express our truest thoughts and feelings right here at school, which is, for now, the center of our lives.'"

The students roared with cheers. Rod and Belinda seemed stunned.

"And now," Mads said, "I would like to show you why the 1972 yearbook was censored." She clicked again. Up it came, blown up huge: the 1972 class picture. The moon shot, larger than life.

The crowd screamed and shrieked with laughter and shock. Belinda Crocker turned red.

"I admire the class of 1972 what they did in this photo," Mads said. "They made an important point. Maybe you parents have forgotten what it was like to be our age. But you were once like us—passionate about important issues. Remember your own high school years. Sometimes we need to do things that look foolish to you—but we can't grow up without these experiences. Reinstate the Dating Game and let us be our whole, weird, goofy, free, crazy selves!"

The students in the crowd roared. Mads, Lina, and Holly left the stage. The students started chanting, "Mad-i-son! Mad-i-son!"

Lina, Holly, and Mads jumped up and down in a group hug. "You were great! You were so great!" Lina and Holly shouted over the noise.

Mads' parents pushed through the crowd to hug and kiss her too. "Good going, Mads," Russell said. "You ought to be a lawyer someday!"

"Please, Dad, anything but that," Mads said, but she grinned. From him, it was a high compliment.

Rod took the mike.

"Settle down, please! Let's settle down. The parents' board will meet in Classroom 104 across the hallway for an emergency meeting—immediately. Everyone else, I urge to you please leave the campus peacefully. You will be apprised of our decision. Thank you!"

He and Belinda hurried off the stage to jeers and boos. Nobody left the room. Everybody wanted to wait and see what would happen in that meeting.

While the board disappeared into the classroom, the students kept chanting. "Dating Game! Dating Game! Bring back the Dating Game! Bring back the Dating Game!"

"The whole school must be here!" Lina said.

"This is amazing!" Holly said. "I think we did it!"

Mads looked at her father. "What do you think will happen?"

"Who knows?" Russell said. "It takes a lot to get people like Rod and Belinda Crocker to change their mind. But whatever happens, you did your best."

Rod reappeared on the stage fifteen minutes later. The rowdy audience cheered. "That was quick," Holly said.

"I have an announcement to make," Rod said. "In light

of the recent arguments made by Madison Markowitz, Holly Anderson, and Lina Ozu, the parents' board has voted to reinstate the Dating Game on the school blog."

The auditorium erupted in happy shouts. "We did it! We did it!" Mads, Lina, and Holly jumped up and down, hugging and holding hands and screaming happily. "Mads, it's all because of you," Holly said.

"I'm so proud of you!" Mads' mother said.

Rod left the stage and approached Mads. "May I see you privately for a moment, Madison?"

Mads followed him out of the auditorium. Rod led her to the relative quiet of an empty classroom.

"Congratulations," he said. "I admire your conviction, your willingness to stand up for what you believe in, and your thorough research skills."

"Thank you."

"I—" He started laughing, then choked out, "I have to admit, that picture is funny."

"And it makes the Dating Game look like kindergarten stuff," Mads said.

"In a way, it does," Rod said. "But remember—the parents' board will be watching you. You have to keep your blog clean. Okay? Don't make me look at that old picture again—I can't take it."

"Okay," Mads said.

"Good. Your suspension is over. Please return to school tomorrow. I will see that this episode is stricken from your record. It won't hurt you in any way."

"Thank you!" Mads nearly jumped up and hugged him, but held herself back.

"You would have fit in well with us back in the old days, Mads," Rod said. "You would have made a great hippie radical. Now go celebrate with your friends."

"Thanks, Mr. Alvarado." *He's really not so rigid, after all,* Mads thought. Maybe he didn't deserve the nickname "Rod." Mads thought maybe she should stop calling him that, even privately. But she knew she wouldn't.

25 Backne Check

To:	linaonme
From:	your daily horoscope

HERE IS TODAY'S HOROSCOPE: CANCER: Your long, winding, painful path has finally brought you your heart's desire. Would it kill you to take the short, straight, pleasant path next time?

Hey, congratulations!" Walker said. Lina, Mads, Holly, Rob, Sebastiano, Ramona, and tons of other kids had flooded the Rutgers Roadhouse, a rock club, Thursday night for a big post-meeting celebration. A band was playing, and the students were in a happy mood, amped on a sense of their own power.

Lina hadn't had a chance to talk to Walker since their kiss. She wondered what was going on—did he regret it?

Did he feel guilty? Did he tell Flynn about it? She looked up at him nervously.

"You guys were amazing," Walker said. "That stuff Mads dug up—she should go into investigative reporting."

"I know," Lina said. "She was fantastic. I'm just glad she can come back to school now and everything's okay."

"Um, look, can I talk to you?" Walker said. He nodded toward the door.

"Sure," Lina said. She followed him outside. What did he want? Maybe he was going to say they couldn't kiss like that again because of Flynn. After all, he did have a girlfriend. . . .

A few kids were smoking in the parking lot. Walker and Lina leaned against a car.

"I just wanted to tell you that I broke up with Flynn," Walker said.

"You did?" Lina stared at her feet, trying not to give away how happy and surprised she felt.

"Uh-huh." He faced her and took both her hands in his. He was shaking. *He's nervous!* Lina realized.

"Lina—I want to be with you," he said. "In a girlfriend/boyfriend way, I mean. More than friends."

"You do?" When she looked into his face, she felt flooded with a warm, happy feeling. Walker! He wanted to be with her! He was her guy! And it seemed right.

"So—what do you think about that?"

"I like it," she said. "I want to be with you, too."

"Really? You're not messing with my head?"

"No—really! I've liked you for a long time," she said. "I was just too stupid to realize it for a while."

"Me too," Walker said. He bent his face toward her. She tilted hers up. They kissed. Their second kiss. It was soft and sweet and better than the first one. Lina sighed and put her arms around him. He pulled her against him and held her close.

Finally she liked someone who liked her back! No more impossible dreams, liking people who were unavailable or taken. He was hers and she was his. She wondered why it had taken her so long to get here. But sometimes that's just the way things go.

We're back! The Dating Game is back on the RSAGE school Web site. Thank you all for your fabulous support! We couldn't have done it without you! Free speech for everyone! And matchmaking forever!

X-Rating

OFFICIAL CORRECTION

A few weeks ago an X-Rating from someone named "Elvira" appeared on this site in error. It contained much false information and never should have been allowed online. First, there is no Elvira; it was a false name. Second, nothing she wrote about her victim, Walker Moore, was true. I repeat: Nothing! We have erased Elvira's X-Rating. I would like to replace it with a Current-Girlfriend Rating.

Your name: *Lina Ozu*

Your grade: *10th*

Your boyfriend's name: *Walker Moore*

Your boyfriend's grade: *11th*

How do you know him/her? *school*

How have you been together? *a day*

What do you think of your boyfriend? *He's patient, honest, smart, a good writer, not as good a speller as he thinks [oh, yeah? Prove it! -WM], a little quick-tempered, and really, really cute.*

On a scale of 1 to 10, with 10 being the highest, you rate your ex boyfriend: *10 plus*

And for the record, Lina wrote, stopping to peek down the back of Walker's shirt—and, she noticed, he let her—*he doesn't have backne.*

Here's a sneak peek at *The Dating Game #5*

"That dirty little punk," Mads said.

"He's not exactly little," Holly said.

"Okay," Mads corrected herself. "That big, weird-haired dork. I always thought his hair looked like it was sewn onto his scalp."

"*Now* you tell me," Holly said. They were talking about Rob, Holly's boyfriend—make that *ex*-boyfriend—whose hair was so thick, it looked like teddy bear fur. Unlike Mads (news to Holly), Holly had always loved his hair. *Uh-oh—tears coming on*. Holly pinched her forearm to suppress them. Once they started coming, it was hard to stop.

"We're sympathy-trashing him," Lina said. "For your sake. Doesn't it make you feel better?"

"Not really," Holly said.

"You should go online and X-Rate him right now," Mads said. "Really give it to him so no girl will want to come within five miles of him. He won't get another girlfriend until he's thirty!"

"That's abusing the system," Holly said. "And, anyway, Rob doesn't deserve it. I don't think. I haven't quite sorted out my feelings yet."

Mads reached into the shopping bag she'd brought with her to Holly's house and pulled out three pints of ice cream. "Let's get down to business. We've got Strawberry-Banana Happiness-in-a-Tub, Mint-Chocolate Love-Substitute, and Intense Chocolate Brainwash to chocolatize your troubles away."

Lina dropped *her* shopping bag on Holly's kitchen island. "And I've got cheese popcorn, Cheez Doodles, and Wheat Thins, in case you get a salt jones," she said.

"I'll start with the hard stuff," Holly said, reaching for the Chocolate Brainwash. "Thanks for coming over, you guys. I was almost on the verge of tears there, for a minute."

"The *verge* of tears?" Mads picked up a soggy pile of used Kleenex and tossed it in the trash.

"You heard me." Holly was playing the tough guy, though she knew Mads and Lina saw through it. It made her feel better to pretend she wasn't hurt.

"I still can't believe he dumped you," Lina said. "After all you went through with him! After he begged you to be in his sister's wedding—"

"—and she made you wear that heinous bridesmaid's dress—" Mads said.

"—and you practically planned the whole thing for her," Lina said.

"Not to mention all the swim meets you went to," Mads said. "We *all* went to. Cheering him on like a bunch of cheer-bots."

"Rob should be shunned for this," Lina said. "Ostracized from the community. Like the Amish do when somebody breaks the rules."

"It's not that bad," Holly said. "He has his reasons."

"Like what?" Lina asked.

"Well, he said he was so busy with swimming—"

"Lame."

"—and school—"

"Lame."

"—and studying for the SATs—"

"Totally lame."

"—and dealing with his parents' divorce—"

"Please."

"—that he doesn't have time to be in a relationship right now," Holly finished.

"Yeah? Well, who doesn't have to deal with school and activities and parental insanity?" Mads said. "We're all busy."

"You have to make time for love," Lina said.

"Well, that's what he told me," Holly said. "He said, 'You're a cool girl, I'm really into you, we've had fun, but I don't think I can spend as much time with you as you'd like, so maybe we should be friends.' Then he played this old Bob Dylan song I used to hear at his father's house. You know—the one that goes, 'No, no, no, it ain't me, babe, it ain't me you're looking for, babe'?"

"Ugh," Lina said.

"Like father, like son," Mads said.

"It was a total shock." Holly's tough-guy act was breaking down. She was getting teary again. She didn't have the strength to stop it. "I never saw it coming. I thought everything was fine. I thought we were in love!" She started full-on crying. It was the surprise that bothered her the most. She'd thought she had everything under control. Then Rob pulled the rug out from under her. That scared her. If it could happen once, would her next boyfriend do the same thing? How could she protect herself? And worse, what if she never found another boyfriend?

Mads and Lina hugged her. Mads passed her a handful of Kleenex. "You'll be okay," Lina said.

"You're better off without him," Mads said.

"You're too good for him," Lina said. "You can do way better."

"I know that," Holly said. "But it still hurts."

"You know what you need?" Mads said. "Nothing helps you forget a guy like another guy."

"I don't know," Holly said. "I'm kind of sick of guys."

"You're just sick of *Rob*," Mads said. "He represents all guys to you. But he's just a lower form of guy. There are higher forms to be found."

"Please," Holly said. "What percentage of the total male population could be a higher life-form? It must be tiny, like two percent."

"Maybe five percent," Lina said.

"All right, if you want to be optimistic," Holly said. "Five percent. So out of all the guys at RSAGE, there are maybe—*maybe*—twenty good ones. And at least two of them are taken—by you." Lina and Mads were both enjoying happy times with their new boyfriends, Walker and Stephen. "What are the chances that I'm going to bond with one of the few higher life-forms left?"

"You could date outside of school," Mads said. "That gives you much better chances."

"But how will I meet a guy who doesn't go to our school?" Holly asked. "And even if I meet someone, it takes time to figure out if I like him and he likes me and if he's a decent person or if he's got bodies buried in his backyard. . . ." She dropped her head on the kitchen counter and moaned. "I'm doomed. I'll never have another boyfriend as long as I live! The odds are just too low!"

"That's ridiculous," Lina said. "It feels that way now, but you'll find a new guy before you know it."

"What if we speed things up?" Mads said. "Like, what if you could meet twenty guys at once? Wouldn't it be great if you could go to a party and every guy there was available? And you could spend the whole party flirting and talking and by the time it was over, all you had to do was choose one?"

"Sure, it would," Holly said. "I'd also like to be Prince William's girlfriend, but it's not going to happen."

"Don't say that!" Mads cried. "I need my illusions. I'm still clinging to that one."

"Mads is onto something," Lina said. "We could hold our own party, singles only. You can casually see how you like the guys without having to go on a million blind dates. And you don't have to worry that you're wasting time flirting with some guy who already has a girlfriend."

"A speed dating party!" Mads said. "You get a certain amount of time—say, ten minutes—to talk to each guy, and by the end of the party, you get matched with the one you like best."

"Who also likes you," Lina said.

"No muss, no fuss," Mads said.

"I guess it could be fun," Holly said.

"We'll open it up to kids from other schools," Mads said. "You're bound to meet a new guy that way."

"And if you don't, we'll just keep having parties until you find The One," Lina said. "It's perfect for busy students. You'll only lose an hour or two a week on it."

"Let's do it." Holly straightened up, some of her old moxie returning. The memory of Rob's teddy-bear head, which had been making her cry all morning, was fading already. "Even if I don't meet a guy right away, it would be fun to make some friends at other schools. The RSAGE social scene could use some new life. New parties! New people! All right! I'm psyched."

"Yay!" Mads clapped. "Speed dating!"

"I was getting kind of sick of Rob, anyway," Holly said. "I just didn't realize it."

"You're a quick healer. I guess we won't be needing this anymore." Lina started putting the ice cream in the freezer.

"Hey, where are you going with that?" Holly said. "I may be on the mend, but I need to make sure I'm one hundred percent cured. Right?"

"Absolutely," Mads said. "Keep that Chocolate Brainwash coming."

Don't miss a minute of
THE DATING GAME
WITH Holly, Madison, and Lina!

Read them all!

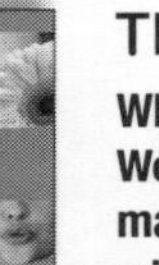

THE DATING GAME

When Holly, Madison, and Lina's Dating Game Web site class project is a hit, they become the matchmaking masters of their school. But how will it affect their own lives?

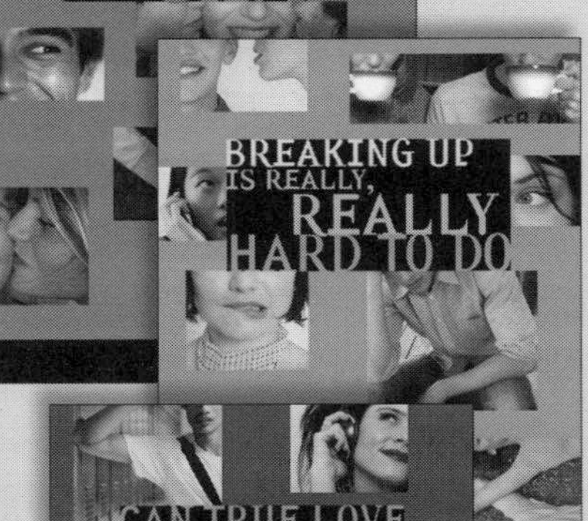

BREAKING UP IS REALLY, REALLY HARD TO DO

In Book Two, the girls' love lives get even more complicated. Lina, Madison, and Holly each think they have an "IT" guy… until Stephen comes along. Then Madison wonders, can there be two "Its"?

CAN TRUE LOVE SURVIVE HIGH SCHOOL?

Sometimes love lasts forever, but not always. Holly, Madison, and Lina's lives get even more complex with broken hearts, betrayals, and, most dangerous of all, college boys entering the scene!

The only game where the rules keep changing!

Log on to

www.DatingGameBook.com

for much more